Ten Days in Town

Three Rivers Ranch Romance™
Book 9

Liz Isaacson

ISBN-13: 978-1-63876-337-6

"Delight thyself also in the Lord; and he shall give thee the desires of thine heart."

PSALMS 37:4

Chapter One

The dates Sandy Keller had been on hadn't been so disastrous in at least six months. Maybe longer. She'd been out with so many men, she'd lost count. Of course, she hadn't ever had to drive out to Three Rivers Ranch to pick up her date before. That was a new low.

And so was having him say the words "my girl-friend" while *she* paid for dinner.

She fumed as she pulled into the parking lot, the long drive of shame back from the ranch finally over. Sandy didn't want to return to the pancake house, where she'd have to explain to the night manager how utterly ridiculous dating in Three Rivers had become.

"Only for you," she muttered as she turned the corner and headed toward the back building. Her oasis away from everything, her condo sat around the rear of the building, giving her unprecedented views of the western range. Living on the very edge of town had its perks, she supposed.

She pressed the brake too hard, jerking her car to a stop. Someone had parked in her designated space. Again.

Muttering, she backed up and found an uncovered parking spot, eyeing the red SUV like it had done her a personal wrong. She unlocked her front door and eased into her condo like she was settling into a warm bath.

Coming home had always brought her comfort. So had cooking. She whipped out a batch of oatmeal chocolate chip cookies, slid the tray into the oven, and disappeared into her bedroom to change. She wished she could slip away from the night's horrors as easily as she shed one set of clothes and replaced them with silky pajamas.

She looked at herself in the bathroom mirror, trying to see her flaws. Oh, she had them—a lot of them —but she couldn't understand why everyone around her seemed to be able to find someone to love and she couldn't.

"No more dating anyone from the ranch," she told her reflection.

Sure, she'd been on some fun dates with some nice guys. But she hadn't made it past the third date in over a year. There had to be something wrong with her, but looking at her brown eyes and highlighted brown hair, she couldn't see it.

So, like she'd done dozens of times before, she returned to the kitchen to drown out the memories of her terrible date in ooey gooey chocolate.

The timer beeped once as she came out of her bedroom—the signal that it had been going off for a while. Her adrenaline spiked. How long had she been staring at herself in the mirror?

Thin, white smoke issued from the vents at the rear of the oven. She hurried into the kitchen, grabbed the oven mitts from the drawer, and yanked open the door.

Smoke and heat and vapor smacked her in the face. She cringed and pulled back, her stomach rioting over the loss of the cookies.

She'd barely slammed the ruined sheet of what was going to be her saving grace for the night on the stovetop when someone opened her front door.

Panic poured through her in waves, and she lifted her still oven-mitted hands like she could ward off any attack with them.

"Sandy?" a man asked.

Through the haze, Sandy made out the tall form of her brother, Hank. Relief made her sag against the peninsula. Just as quickly, she straightened and marched into the living room. "What are you doing here?"

Hank lifted his duffle bag. "We're here for the holidays." He peered at her, something he had to do to actually see her through the smoke hanging in the air. "Did you forget Ma was gettin' new floors done this week?" He gestured to someone standing behind him. "You said me and Tad could stay here."

Sandy tried to see her brother's best friend from college, but he lingered directly behind Hank. "I did say that." She stepped back. "Come on in. I haven't gotten the beds made up yet. Weren't you coming tomorrow?"

"Willow's coming in tomorrow."

Of course. Willow, Hank's bubbly, blonde girlfriend. Well, fiancé now that he'd asked her to marry him. Sandy's only comfort all these years had been that Hank hadn't been able to get married either. She hadn't been the only disappointment to her mother. But come June, she would be.

Hank stepped into the living room, finally revealing Tad. He flashed a mega watt grin that made Sandy's heart go flippity-flop and stepped forward. "Sandy, it's so good to see you again."

She stared at his outstretched hand, not quite sure if she trusted herself to shake it. Seconds stretched into awkwardness, which Hank broke by saying, "Don't you own the pancake house now? How is it possible for you to burn cookies?"

Embarrassment flooded Sandy's cheeks, along with a healthy dose of heat. She turned away from Tad's tall frame, his intoxicating dark eyes, which still watched her, his windswept, dark chocolate-colored hair. She'd met him a few times in the past, only for a couple of minutes. But now he screamed *available!* even though she'd just sworn off dating.

You just swore off dating anyone living at the ranch, she amended as she went to open the windows in the dining room. *And Tad doesn't live out at the ranch.*

She gave herself a mental shake, a stern reminder not to be ridiculous. Tad was going to be here for ten days, not forever. And Sandy, owner of the steady and successful pancake house, was a lifetime resident of Three Rivers. The thought had never felt like such a life sentence.

Tad Jorgensen watched Sandy Keller—his best friend's little sister—slink into the dining room to open windows. He'd left the front door open, but not because he'd thought it would help clear out the gauzy smoke. But because Sandy's beauty had struck him full in the chest, rendering him slow of thought. It had been a miracle he'd managed to say hello and offer his hand to her.

She hadn't taken it, and now he focused on his fingers, thinking them covered with slime or something.

Sandy's light laugh brought Tad out of his trance. His pulse quickened when she glanced his way, and he needed to pull himself together. Fast. He'd come up with a plausible reason he could go home for Christmas with Hank this year when he'd never been able to before. Mandatory vacation.

Helicopter pilots rarely got vacation, especially in the tourist industry where Tad worked. *Used to work,* he thought as he watched Sandy and Hank banter in the kitchen. His fingers itched to touch her silky pajamas, and he reined in his thoughts.

She's your best friend's sister, he told himself. *And you're unemployed.*

Even if she had burnt the cookies, she wouldn't be interested in a helicopter pilot who was afraid to fly.

Bitterness, now becoming more and more familiar as the weeks passed, coated his throat. He had been asked to take a mandatory vacation over the holidays— usually the busiest time of the year—but it wasn't because he'd stored up too many days.

He forced his mind somewhere—anywhere—else, and the traitorous thing landed back on Sandy.

"Didn't think you'd be here," Hank said when

Tad's brain started working again. "That's why I opened the door without knocking."

"Why wouldn't I be here?" Sandy sat at her bar, her back to Tad, but he heard the false note in her voice.

"You said you had a date." Hank pinned her with an older brother look that said *Well, why aren't you out?*

Sandy's shoulders fell, and her chin dipped for half a beat. It could've been Tad's imagination, but he swore she angled her face in his direction when she said, "I'm not really into dating right now. I have the pancake house to whip into shape and...." He let her sentence hang there, and Tad wasn't sure if she didn't know how to finish it or just didn't want to in mixed company.

Hank frowned, his confusion evident. "I thought you liked—"

"Hank," she warned. "So, which of you wants my office?" She stood and faced Tad fully. Again, the subtle strength in her face, the set of her shoulders hit Tad in a way it never had before. An edge of sadness also rode in her expression, barely noticeable. In fact, Tad wondered if anyone else would be able to see it. Or if he could because the same vein of despair had been lingering with him since the beginning of

November, when he'd barely made it back to the rim of the Grand Canyon.

In many ways, he was still out there. Still lost in the wilderness. Still radioing for help.

His clients hadn't filed any complaints. Their version of what had happened painted him in a complimentary light. But everything about Tad's confidence had been shattered. He'd thought he understood his helicopter; he'd been flying over the Grand Canyon for years. But nothing had prepared him and no experience could've helped him during that fateful flight.

"Tad?" Sandy stood in front of him now, but he hadn't seen her move.

"I'll take the office," Tad said. "Sure." He glanced left and right, seeing only one door to the right of the kitchen. That would be her room. On the left, an arched doorway revealed a hall branching in both directions, with a closed door at the junction. He stepped that way.

"I can set up my own bed. Or sleep on the couch. The floor. Whatever." He didn't want to add to Sandy's load. She looked and sounded a bit worn down.

His attention came back to her when she said, "Let me clean up in there first," with a tremor of trepidation in her tone.

He paused upon entering the hall. Her office obviously existed to his right, but he didn't want to enter it unless she approved. "Sure. Is this the bathroom?"

"Yeah." Sandy squeezed behind him and entered the office. "I'll just be a minute." She closed the door, that panicked edge in her eye kicking Tad's pulse into a new gear.

He turned away, frustrated with himself. He could not be attracted to Hank's little sister, even if she was twenty-seven years old. Tad joined Hank in the kitchen, where he stood at the sink, staring out the window.

"Three Rivers," he said, though darkness had fallen an hour ago and not much could be seen.

"So much sky," Hank added, and Tad appreciated being able to see something in a way Las Vegas had never allowed. He could see the stars without straining. Coming into town, Tad had felt the smallness of it, and something about it sang to his soul.

He hadn't told anyone about the flight that had almost ended his life, and had definitely stalled his career.

"So what's here?" he asked Hank.

Hank shrugged and turned away from the window. "Small town stuff." He spoke as if small towns had nothing to offer. But Tad craved the tranquility and peace of a place like Three Rivers. Somewhere where no one knew him, no one thought of him as a helicopter pilot, no one assumed anything about him.

Stay, he thought, and the feeling spread through him slowly, like honey dripping from the hive. Tad closed his eyes and drank in the peace emanating from the very air in Three Rivers.

He was going to stay—and not just for the ten days with Hank. But for good.

His decision made, and approved of by the Lord, Tad couldn't wait to spend some time alone. Because now he needed to figure out what he could do in Three Rivers to make a living.

Chapter Two

Sandy opened the bottom drawer in her desk and shoved in anything that would fit inside. The computer and desk dominated the room, but she'd also put in a deluxe sleeper sofa that would accommodate Tad's height just fine. She just didn't want him to see the mess she worked in. She'd been planning to clean her office before the New Year, but owning and figuring out and running the pancake house took a lot of her time.

In short, she needed a vacation. She fired off a text to Gail, her front-of-the-house manager, asking her if she could manage the pancake house alone the following day. Sandy had unfolded the couch and set the air pump to blow up the airbed before she got a response.

Definitely, Gail said. *It'll be slow until the New*

Year's Eve pancake fundraiser. Take all the time off you want.

Every muscle in Sandy's body sighed. She wanted to take off the next eight days until New Year's Eve, but she knew she wouldn't. But she would sleep in tomorrow, and go to lunch with her brother, and welcome Willow, and eat dinner with her family. The thoughts comforted her, brought a smile to her face where one hadn't been in a while.

With the natural disaster that had been her desk contained, and the bed ready, she stepped into the hall to get sheets. She couldn't see Tad, but his presence filled her condo. And it called to her.

Confused, she opened the linen closet and collected the things she needed. She'd flapped the fitted sheet once when Tad said, "I'll help you."

The hair on the back of her neck stood at attention as he moved behind her and around to the other side of the bed.

"Thanks for letting us stay here," he said, taking one corner of the sheet.

"Sure, yeah." Sandy wanted to pull the words back into her throat. "You still flying?" She tugged her corner over the edge of the mattress and glanced at him.

He'd frozen completely, his gaze that same faraway, here but not here, look she'd seen in the living room several minutes ago. Sandy had seen this look before, usually on the face of Pete Marshall or Reece Sanders. Men who had seen horrific things and somehow survived. But Tad hadn't served in the military.

Sandy sidestepped down to the other corner, glad when Tad moved with her.

"I'm...." He exhaled as he pulled on his end of the sheet. "Yeah. Still flying."

She detected something strange in his voice and glanced up. His gorgeous eyes hooked hers. She sank into them even though she commanded herself not to. The air in the room turned charged and something sparked between her and Tad in a way it never had before.

She imagined climbing into his helicopter with him and just flying. Flying anywhere but here. Flying fast and furious until they ran out of fuel and had to land. And wherever that was would be amazing, because it wasn't here.

Startled by the depth of her fantasy, Sandy blinked and reminded herself of her reality. Sure, she could take a few days off work. She would. Maybe she'd be able to find her center. Re-start her passion for the restaurant business. Rejuvenate herself for another year of solitude.

Tad tossed the flat sheet onto the bed, and Sandy used the distraction to force herself to focus on the situation in front of her. She couldn't afford to let herself slip into daydreams and self-depreciating thoughts. Hank rivaled her mother in his detective skills, and he'd know something was bothering Sandy before bedtime.

"Fly anywhere fun recently?" she asked.

"Just the Grand Canyon."

Sandy grabbed the pillows and placed them on the bed. She reached for the quilt and together, she and Tad finished making the bed.

"Thanks," she said. "You still live in Vegas?"

He dropped to the bed and studied the floor. "Yep."

Sandy suddenly found the conversation too one-sided. He hadn't asked her a single question, and he didn't seem terribly forthcoming about his answers. "Okay." She took a step backward. "I'm going to make sure Hank's room is ready, and then I'm going to try those cookies again. You're welcome anywhere."

He lifted his hand as she left and went in the guest room opposite of his. This room held a queen bed, already made up for guests. Sandy didn't have anyone stay very often, but everything here was clean and ready. She returned to the living room to tell Hank and found him fast asleep in the recliner.

He had come from a different time zone, but eight-thirty was early for bed no matter what. Sandy admired her brother, her heart full at his presence. She lifted his duffle and placed it inside the guest room before heading into the kitchen to recreate the chocolatey treat she desperately needed.

Help me get them right this time, she prayed as she whipped butter and brown sugar. God surely didn't care how her cookies turned out, but Sandy recalled the thought. Pastor Scott had said that God was interested in their lives, even the little things. That He wanted us to be happy and to pray for what was important—even if that was a batch of cookies.

Sandy calmed as she added eggs and vanilla, then flour, oats and baking soda, and finally the chocolate chips. She sat at her dining room table while they baked, her thumbs firing off texts to Gail and a couple other key members of her staff.

"Can I join you?"

Sandy startled, though Tad's voice vibrated gently against her eardrums.

"Sure, of course." She placed her phone face-down on the table so she could give him her full attention.

Don't ask him another question, she coached herself. *Do not ask him anything.*

But he didn't speak, and the clicking of her oven and Hank's steady breathing almost drove her mad.

Just when Sandy was about to blurt the first thing that came to her mind, Tad said, "So I was looking at something on my phone." He tilted it toward her. "What's this Bowman's Champion Breeds?"

Being a small town, having someone new in town piqued everyone's interest. And Brynn Bowman, a world champion barrel racer, had caused quite the stir when she'd moved to Three Rivers over the summer.

"It's a horse-training facility," Sandy said. "Brynn Bowman is a champion barrel racer. She's going to be training champion horses for the rodeo."

"This says they're gearing up to open."

"Yeah, that's probably right." Sandy didn't want to pry, but she didn't understand why Tad cared about a horse-training facility out on the ranch. He was about as far from a cowboy as a man could get—and her attraction to him ratcheted up another notch because of it.

Tad cocked his head and stared at her. "You working tomorrow?"

She squinted at him. "I was actually planning to take the day off."

That delicious grin spread his lips, causing her to focus on his mouth. Her fantasies ran wild, all of them ending with a kiss with Tad.

"Maybe you can take me out to the ranch to see this place." He glanced at his phone and back to her. "I want to check it out."

Sandy's heart settled like a stone. The last thing

she wanted to do was return to Three Rivers Ranch, especially after tonight's disaster. Never going there again sounded like a better idea.

"Really?" she asked. "What do you think you're going to do at a place like that? What if it's not even open?"

"I just want to check it out," Tad said, his voice that false airy type that Sandy had heard a lot of people use when they were lying. "I'm sure there's an office or something, at least."

"You don't seem like the cowboy type," she said, pushing the issue.

"I don't?" He lifted his eyebrows before smiling. "Yeah, I guess not. Maybe Hank will let me borrow one of his old hats."

"I've got a couple," Sandy said, pushing her chair back.

"You've got a couple of men's cowboy hats?"

Sandy froze, halfway turned toward the front entrance closet. What could she tell him? That yes, she had a couple of men's cowboy hats because she'd purchased them for gifts and then the guy had broken up with her? That she was too busy serving coffee and pancakes to return them?

She might as well outline how pathetic she was.

Thankfully, the timer went off on the oven, signaling the cookies were done. She turned that way instead, and forced a giggle through stiff lips. "Oh, right. Mine are for ladies." She pulled the cookies out of the oven, the desire to eat the dozen by herself raging within her.

"So, will you take me out there tomorrow? Willow is coming in, and I'm sure Hank will want to be here to introduce her to your parents."

"I'm sure," Sandy murmured as she finished moving the cookies from the sheet pan to the cooling rack. "And why not? I'll take you out to the ranch tomorrow." She twisted and jabbed the spatula toward him. "But I'm sleeping in."

Tad's grin nearly melted her insides. Sandy thought she'd never need to find comfort in the arms of another chocolate chip cookie if she had him to come home to every day.

"This says they don't open until ten," he said. "Does that work?"

She picked up a warm cookie, pleased at how perfect this batch had turned out. "As long as we *leave* at ten. It's a forty-minute drive." She pointed to the cookies. "Want one?"

"These do look better than the last batch."

"Ha ha." Her natural instinct was to slap playfully at his impressive bicep, especially after his flirtatious statement and delivery. But she snatched up another cookie instead. She couldn't flirt with Tad.

Could she?

Her feelings swirled like a tornado, and by the time they'd eaten their way through most of the cookies, the conversation lighter and easier, Sandy felt wrung out. She escaped to her bedroom at the same time Tad did, Hank still snoring softly in the recliner.

She fell into bed since she already wore her pajamas. And though her mind felt bruised from all it had been through today, the one shining ray was Tad.

THE NEXT MORNING, Tad felt like he was gearing up to take a group of tourists over the deepest part of the Grand Canyon. Though he'd been flying for a decade, the nervous buzz of bees in his gut never went away. Not until he brought them all back to the rim safely.

But he was nowhere near the canyon now, and he'd already decided to give up piloting completely. So as he brushed his teeth and combed his hair, he couldn't quite figure out why he felt like he could fall off a cliff at any moment.

He stepped out of the bathroom and put his toiletry bag in his suitcase. Behind him and around the corner, he heard the low warble of Sandy's voice as she bustled around the kitchen. His nerves rioted, and everything became clear.

Tad had always craved an adrenaline rush—it was what got him into flying helicopters in the first place. He actually enjoyed the tremors in his stomach, lived for the rush of hovering over the Green River and doing a buzz by Hoover Dam.

And now, everything in him wanted to see Sandy, smell Sandy, and get closer to Sandy. He smoothed his palms down his jeans as he went into the kitchen, expecting to see her fresh from bed, maybe without makeup and just getting ready to shower.

Instead, she stood in front of the French doors that led to her small balcony, her back to him. Her dark hair cascaded down her back in soft curls he wanted to run his fingers through. He fisted his hands, wondering if his attraction to her would be approved of by her brother.

Tad glanced over his shoulder, but Hank's door stayed shut. Maybe what Hank didn't know didn't need to hurt him. And why would Tad dating Sandy hurt Hank? Tad was a good guy, even if he was currently unemployed and not telling anyone why.

She wore a long-sleeved, green sweater and a pair of jeans that hugged every curve. Tad cleared his throat and forced his attention to the coffee maker. Sandy turned and nearly sent his adrenaline to the moon with her dazzling smile.

"Morning," she said. "You just put in one of those

pods." She pointed to the counter. "Choose the flavor you want. Pop it in, hit brew."

He reached for one of the disposable pods she'd indicated. He chose a regular roast and stuck it in the machine. He selected one of the mugs she'd set on the counter so he wouldn't try to touch her and set the coffee to brew. "Thought you said you were sleeping in."

She sighed and added a little giggle at the end that made a thrill squirrel up Tad's spine. "I can never sleep in. I used to work the breakfast shift at the pancake house." She met his eye. "Old habit."

"So you don't go in for breakfast anymore?"

"I'm really that transparent, huh?"

"It's eight o'clock," he said. "You said we couldn't even leave till ten." He shrugged and added a scoop of sugar to his coffee.

"Yeah, I'm usually at the house at six," she said. "I stay through lunch, because my night manager comes in at three."

Tad returned her natural smile. He'd already asked her if she liked owning the pancake house. She'd claimed to love it, and going in at six a.m. testified further of that. Standing there with her, sipping coffee that desperately needed a shot of hazelnut cream, Tad couldn't think of a single thing to say. He just liked being with Sandy. The quaking in his gut had gone out, and he didn't feel the need to stuff this silence with awkward questions.

The urge to tell her he'd quit flying surged to the front of Tad's brain. The words sat on the edge of his tongue. But she'd already asked if he was still flying, and he'd said he was. He'd been in Three Rivers for twelve hours. Talked with Sandy for maybe two. He barely knew her, even if he felt comfortable with her.

"Maybe we can go get some pancakes," he said. "Since you didn't want to leave until ten and all. I'd like to see your house."

A sparkled entered her eye. "You really want to?"

Tad took a step closer, his eyes seemingly unable to look anywhere but into hers. Dozens of lines ran through his mind, but he managed to say, "Sure, why not?" casually, like he wasn't aching to see what the pancake house had to say about Sandy Keller.

"I'll wake Hank."

Tad's spirits fell, and he hid his emotion behind his coffee mug. Sandy flounced out of the kitchen while Tad wondered—again—why he thought getting to know his best friend's little sister was a good idea.

He'd barely swallowed another mouthful of coffee when Sandy returned. "Hank's picking Willow up in Amarillo at eleven. He can't come." Her fingers worried themselves around each other. "Then he's taking her to lunch in the city before coming back out here." Her gaze flitted around the room. "I guess he'll be back around four. My mother's making Christmas Eve dinner, something she's never done before." A measure of bitterness accompanied her words.

"Ham, I heard," Tad said, cursing himself for not saying something more soothing, more comforting. "It's totally overrated. Turkey is a much better Christmas meat."

Stop talking! he commanded himself, but Sandy smiled at him.

"I totally think turkey should be eaten at Christmas," she said. "My mom always dries out the ham."

An opportunity bloomed in Tad's mind. "Well, let's eat as many pancakes as we can now." He offered her his arm, surprised at himself and even more shocked when she slipped her hand into the crook of his elbow. Though he wore his jacket already, fire came with the weight of her arm in his. He tucked her close, unsure of what the heck he was doing.

"And then we can get lunch too," he finished. "You need your purse or anything?"

"It's in my car."

"You leave your purse in your car?"

"It's Three Rivers." She opened the door. "You grew up in a small town, Tad. You know how it is."

He did, so he nodded, but he was drunk on the

sound of her voice saying his name. He went with her down the steps and to a red sedan.

"Someone parked in my spot," she said, glancing down the row of cars. "Looks like they're gone now."

"Does that happen a lot?"

"More than I'd like."

"And yet you leave your purse in the car." He scoffed and chuckled at the same time. "Sounds like Three Rivers isn't all it's cracked up to be."

She swatted his arm, and he pulled her closer to his side. She paused, and he did too, and time seemed to as well. Sandy looked up at him, and he looked down at her, and Tad knew in that moment that the attraction he felt for her wasn't one-sided.

"Tad," she said.

He waited for her to continue. When she didn't, he took a deep breath and forced reason into his thoughts. Adding a smile to his actions, he stepped away from her, veering toward the passenger side of her car. She unlocked it, the sharp sound of the locks breaking the moment—and the awkwardness—between them.

He folded himself into her tiny car and buckled up, keeping his focus away from her by training his eyes out the window. "This is a beautiful town," he said.

"I guess."

"You guess?" He dared a quick look at her but couldn't read her expression so fast.

"I've...." She pulled out of the parking lot and Tad couldn't help himself. He stared at her, troubled by the long pause and the crease between her eyebrows.

She pulled onto the road, pointing the car east. "I've lived here my whole life." Her fingers flexed on the steering wheel.

"Ah." Tad remembered his teenage feelings of being trapped in the small Wyoming town of Stillwater, where nothing ever happened and nothing was worth staying for. He'd left as fast as he could and only returned to visit a couple of times a year. He'd completed his pilot training in Los Angeles, and chosen a job in another big city. He loved the activity, the constant noise, the eclectic mix of people.

Or at least he had.

Now, the thought of six hundred thousand people surrounding him brought a panicked edge to Tad's thoughts he couldn't rationalize. Tall buildings reminded him that he could fall. That he was human. That his life could end with simple decisions like feathering the throttle when he should've given it more gas.

He pushed the memories of that flight from his mind.

"You okay?" Sandy's hand landed on his arm. There, then gone. Quick as a wink. But the weight of it pressed into him, burned into his veins. He wanted to reach for her hand, have skin to skin contact.

"Fine," he forced through a narrow throat.

Sandy frowned, but smoothed over it a moment later. "Okay, well, we're here." She gestured out the windshield.

Tad's stomach revolted. How long had he disappeared inside his memories? Too long. Just like he'd done for weeks now. Months, if he were being honest.

Be honest.

The words sounded in his head like a siren, and he shifted so he faced Sandy. "I'm not really okay." The raw emotion in his voice scared him.

Sandy blinked, her eyes softening. She reached across the console and took one of his hands in both of hers. Through Tad's panic and fear, a jolt of electricity came with the touch.

"Well, let's go get a short stack and talk about it." She released his hand as fast as she'd taken it and opened the door.

Tad took a deep drag of her perfume-scented car, unsure of where the conversation would lead but desperate to have it at the same time. He'd only ever really talked about the flight with his boss, and even then it was all logistics. Not how the experience had changed Tad.

But changed him, it had. He stood, glanced around at the brilliant December sky of Texas, and closed his eyes. *Thank you, Lord.*

When he opened his eyes, Sandy waited for him near the hood, her expression concerned but not judgmental. "You ready?"

"Ready," he said. For what, he wasn't quite sure, but his word almost sounded like a promise.

Chapter Three

Sandy knew something wasn't quite right with Tad. She'd known it last night too. Curiosity tugged at her, and she tried to dismiss it. Just because she was small-town didn't mean she had to enjoy gossip.

The bell on the door rang as she entered, and Gail froze her to the spot with a withering glare. "What are you doing here? You took the day off." Her eyes traveled to Tad as he stepped beside Sandy. A knowing glint entered her expression.

"Two today," Sandy said, sending a strong *don't ask anything. Say nothing* vibe to Gail. She didn't usually bring her dates to the pancake house, but Tad wasn't a date. Not even close. More like an old friend who'd be in town for a few days. Nothing more.

She paraded these thoughts through her mind as

Gail led them to the back corner, near the windows she knew Sandy loved. "Coffee?" she asked.

"Yeah," Tad said. "Do you have hazelnut cream?"

"Sure thing, honey." Gail left, taking some of the anxiety Sandy had spooling inside her. She shrugged out of her jacket and sat, pleased when Tad waited until she did to take his own seat.

"Hazelnut cream?" she asked. "That doesn't seem very Vegas."

"Oh, it's very Vegas," he countered, that playful tease back in his voice. "Dirty sodas and every mix-in you can imagine. Soda bars are everywhere. Can't go anywhere and just get a Pepsi. No ma'am. That doesn't fly."

Sandy tipped her head back and laughed. She liked this side of Tad, the one that wasn't burdened with a secret worry. One that didn't censor himself. One that glowed with life.

Amber, one of Sandy's best waitresses, brought their coffee, complete with the hazelnut cream. "Y'all ready to order?"

"Pancakes," Tad said. "Lots of them."

"Two tall stacks," Sandy clarified. "You just want buttermilk?"

"With blueberry syrup," he said. "And bacon. I want a lot of bacon too."

"Bring the man a lot of bacon." Sandy smiled first

at Tad and then at Amber. The girl returned the smile and turned away. Sandy's jovial mood went with her.

"So," she started. "About you disappearing in the middle of a conversation...."

A pained expression shot across Tad's face. "Is that what I do?"

"Twice now." Sandy settled her elbows on the table, like she didn't much care what haunted him. The truth was, she needed to know. Needed to help him.

Why, she wasn't sure. Maybe because someone so handsome shouldn't be so troubled. But Sandy dismissed the idea. She'd been attracted to a lot of handsome men. She'd dated many of them. She'd never felt this need to help them, soothe them, smooth out the rough parts of their pasts.

Maybe it was because Tad was Hank's friend, and she knew what kind of man he'd used to be.

"I don't like flying," he blurted. His eyes caught hers and wouldn't let go. Sandy tried to read what swam in their dark depths but couldn't quite grasp what she saw.

"You've always loved flying." She wished she didn't sound so strangled, but her dreams of jumping onto a helicopter with Tad and jetting off to destinations unknown fizzled.

They were stupid fantasies anyway, she scolded herself. She always managed to come up with some harebrained idea of romance, of how a relationship with a particular man would go. And when it didn't turn out that way, she ended up alone again, making cookies and going into work in the wee hours of the morning.

Even though Tad had just come into her life, her thoughts had circled an exciting world adventure with him.

He pulled his gaze from hers and stirred his coffee. "Did Hank tell you why I was able to come visit?"

"No." Sandy didn't even think about why Tad had accompanied her brother this time. Hank came home every year between Christmas and New Year's. He'd been at his restaurant in Vegas long enough to get the prime vacation time.

"It's really busy in Vegas this time of year. Lots of tourists." He looked out the window like he meant the words only for himself.

Sandy frowned, trying to match the pieces up. His glazed look. His admission that he didn't like flying. His presence. "What happened with your job?"

He jolted like she'd stabbed him with her fork. Soon enough, he settled back into a peaceful expression, sipping that hazelnut coffee in silence. Sandy decided to emulate him. He'd talk when he was ready.

Amber brought the plates of pancakes and bacon, and Sandy slathered her butter from side to side.

"There was an accident," Tad finally said once Amber had moved away and he'd swallowed a piece of bacon. "At the beginning of November. Flying hasn't been the same since." He cut his pancake into a couple of bites and drizzled blueberry syrup over them. "I haven't been the same."

He speared the pancake and put it in his mouth.

Sandy copied him, but her usually delicious pancakes tasted like sawdust in her mouth. "What kind of accident?" She managed to keep the interest out of her voice, replacing it with compassion. Something tugged in her chest, right against her heart. She liked this broken side of Tad too.

Stop it, she told herself. She'd tried fixing men in the past. All that led to was a heap of resentment and a painful break-up. Besides, she and Tad were friends. Not dating. Not in a relationship.

"My bird malfunctioned. I panicked a little. Did things in the wrong order." The bite he put in his mouth this time would surely choke him. Sandy took it as a sign he didn't want to explain further.

She nibbled on the edge of her pancake—usually her favorite bite because of the crispiness from the grill —and sipped her coffee. She waved Amber away from ten feet so the girl wouldn't interrupt.

"Was anyone hurt?"

He obviously was, but Sandy wasn't quite sure

how. He didn't walk with a limp. She'd only seen him in long sleeves, so he could have scars. Or maybe everything that had happened had left trauma on his mind, his ego, his heart.

"No." He sighed. "That's the thing. I got everyone back to the rim just fine. It was rocky, not gonna lie. But we all made it. No blood. No broken bones. Nothing." He set his fork down as that faraway look relaxed his face and tensed it at the same time. He pressed his lips together and exhaled through his nose.

When Tad brought his gaze back to hers, he carried agony in his eyes. "The clients even said I did everything right." He shook his head. "But I didn't. And the real kicker is I don't know what I should've done differently." He picked up his fork again, pushed his pancakes around in the purple syrup. "And that's what keeps me up at night. It's what paralyzes me when I get in the cockpit." He snatched a piece of bacon and took a bite, glancing around the pancake house. "This place is real nice." He looked at her for a split second, a smile gracing his mouth now. "Feels like you."

Warmth gathered in Sandy's face though his compliment hadn't been terribly overt. He hadn't even really said anything nice about her, specifically. She had put her stamp on the pancake house, closing it for a week while she repainted, and installed new carpet, and updated the light fixtures and décor.

"It's sophisticated," he continued. "But comfortable. Like home."

"Thanks," Sandy said, pleased he found her aesthetic to be exactly what she'd been aiming for. She tried not to let herself read more into what he said than just the words. She'd done that before to her detriment. Her pulse sped against her will, and Sandy leaned back in her chair to put some distance between herself and Tad.

"You finished?" He nodded to her mostly full plate.

"I may have eaten a few cookies before you got up." She pinned him with a mock glare. "Lazybones."

He laughed, the sound morphing him from the serious, traumatized Tad into the carefree, handsome man Sandy felt herself falling for.

"Well, let's go." He pushed his plate away. "Though we haven't eaten nearly enough pancakes to sustain us until lunch."

"I don't cook, I'll have you know." Sandy stood, surprised when Tad rounded the table and helped her into her jacket. The weight and heat of his hands through the fabric sent a bolt of heat down her arms. Her fingers tingled.

"You own a pancake house." He lingered so close

behind her, his breath drifted across her neck. "And those cookies changed my life."

She turned into his arms, a breathless laugh escaping her throat. Her heart rippled like a flag in a stiff Texas wind. He gazed down on her, his expression heated now, matching hers.

"Well, cookies aren't a meal," she managed to say before stepping away. Gail's gaze on Sandy's back felt like a load of bricks, and Sandy would not do something right here in her pancake house she couldn't take back. Couldn't explain. Couldn't maintain.

Because though Tad had just said he didn't like flying, he hadn't said he wasn't going back. Sandy headed for her car, reminding herself that Tad was only in town for a visit. He wasn't going to stay permanently.

The fact made her heart do a double-beat before it settled into its normal rhythm, completely resigned to only enjoying Tad for a few more days.

TAD'S EXCITEMENT grew with every mile that passed between town and the ranch. The openness of the land calmed him, coated his raw nerves in a balm he hadn't known existed. Three Rivers reminded him a lot of Stillwater, but his hometown had never felt so welcoming, or a place where he could be Tad Jorgensen without any strings.

He released a breath and it felt like the invisible band that had been binding his lungs for the past two months had snapped. Finally. A text came just as Sandy turned from asphalt to dirt. He glanced down and caught Chuck's name before the screen darkened. The tension returned, but Tad pushed it back. It felt so good to just breathe, and he didn't want to let that go just yet.

His boss could wait. Probably just checking up on him anyway. Tad wasn't expected to be back until after the New Year.

Sandy rounded the corner, her knuckles so white Tad sensed a storm beneath her happy surface. "I should've rented a car," he said. "Then you wouldn't have to wait for me."

"I don't mind waiting." She pulled up to a large barn sporting a sign that read "Bowman's Champion Breeds."

But she looked like she minded. Sandy stared straight out of the windshield, seeing something besides the innocent barn in front of her.

"I just want to talk to...what did you say her name was?"

"Brynn."

"Brynn." Tad put the name in his memory,

thinking about a girl he knew from Stillwater, whose name was Lynn. Brynn rhymed, and he knew he wouldn't forget. He opened the door and got out of the car.

A winter wind whipped across the range, nipping at his jacket and tousling his hair. He smiled into it. Even the winter in Three Rivers couldn't be nasty. Not really.

A woman opened the door to the barn and leaned into the jamb. "Mornin'," she said. Her dark hair had been contained in a braid that came over her shoulder, and she wore a cowboy hat that threw her face into shadows.

"Are you Brynn Bowman?" Tad stepped forward to shake her hand.

"I am. What can I do for you?"

"I have a few questions about what you do here." Tad glanced around, trying to take in the arenas, the fenced areas, the barns in one single swoop. The inkling of an idea toyed in the back of his mind.

"I train horses to be rodeo champions," Brynn said, looking him up and down. "You ride?"

"Oh, no." Tad chuckled at the very thought. "I'm not into rodeo."

Brynn finally smiled. "I didn't think so."

Tad cocked his head and peered at her as Sandy finally joined him. "What does that mean?"

"It means I can tell who the rodeo boys are," she said. "I can usually peg what event they do." She glanced up. "And you're not even wearin' a hat." She looked at Sandy. "Better hang onto him, Miss Sandy. Three Rivers has a severe shortage of non-cowboys."

Every muscle in Tad's body stiffened. "She's not— we're not—"

Pink stained Brynn's cheeks. "Oh, sorry." She spoke more to Sandy than to Tad.

"I mean, Sandy's great—"

"Better stop while you're ahead." Brynn laughed. "Come on in. If you're not a cowboy, I really want to know what you think I can help you with."

With horror still holding his body hostage, Tad looked helplessly at Sandy. She wore a smile and a mischievous sparkle in her eye. "I *am* pretty great."

"And pretty," he said. "I mean, I think you're pretty and you're great and...." Tad wanted to stuff old socks in his mouth just to get himself to shut up.

Sandy's blush assured him he hadn't messed up too badly. Yet. "So what are you doing here?" she asked as she made to follow Brynn into the barn.

"I need a new job," Tad said. "And my dad raised horses and ran a boarding stable."

Sandy froze. "So you want to work out at the ranch?"

"No." Tad tugged her to get her to move, but she

wouldn't. "Not necessarily. I just want to see what Brynn does here. Maybe I can partner with her."

"But you'd still drive out here to work each day."

"Maybe." Tad tried to see further into the barn, but it looked like all hallways. "I don't know anything yet."

"When do you have to be back in Vegas?"

"January third." Tad swallowed back the confession that he was one text away from quitting. "I just want to explore some options." He reached out and tucked Sandy's highlighted hair behind her ear. "I'm not making any major decisions today."

She leaned into his touch, and Tad wondered if she'd let him kiss her. Right here, in this barn that smelled like sawdust and horseflesh. Tad had never wanted so badly to kiss a woman. And that got his feet moving like nothing ever had.

He could not kiss Hank's sister. Not without at least talking to his friend. Not when he didn't have a future to offer her.

Chapter Four

Sandy smiled and smiled and smiled through dinner. She'd never felt more like a Barbie doll. But Willow was blonde and bubbly and bright—she complimented Hank perfectly. If Tad hadn't been there, Sandy would've dissolved into a puddle of goo by the time they said grace.

As it was, the steadiness of the man beside her kept her in the conversation. Lulled her jealousy back into the dark recesses of her mind. Prompted her to laugh at appropriate times and stay engaged.

But, ugh. Engaged. It was the last thing Sandy wanted on her mind.

Willow flashed her diamond at every opportunity —or maybe it just seemed that way to Sandy. Either way, Sandy's mother and daddy had completely fallen for Willow's charms by the time they took their coffee in the living room.

"Hank, can I talk to you for a second?" Tad's question blindsided Sandy. He wasn't going to join them in the living room? She had to go in there with her parents and Willow alone?

She stared at him, silently pleading for him to offer her his elbow like he'd done a few times today. She hadn't realized how reliant on him she'd become.

"Sure thing." Hank kissed Willow before she proceeded into the living room, like they couldn't ever part without exchanging a kiss first. Sandy nearly rolled her eyes.

But her mind lingered on kissing and if she could share one with Tad. She'd spent the day with him, and it had been one of the best days of her life, bar none. By far one of the better dates she'd had in a couple of years.

The man knew how to talk about real things. Things that mattered. Things that she was interested in. Things beyond ranching and horses, though they did speak of those too. She'd asked him about his daddy's boarding stable and if he actually had liked working there.

He'd admitted that he'd felt trapped in his Wyoming small town. Another thing they had in common. Difference was, he'd left his, and Sandy was still dreaming of a day when she could.

Or maybe she wasn't. Tad strutted into the living room, all smiles, and sat next to her on the loveseat. It almost seemed natural for him to lift his arm and drape it over her shoulders. Almost natural for her to snuggle into his side, take a deep breath, and be happy in his arms.

Sandy wasn't even sure she knew what happiness felt like. When she'd bought the pancake house came to mind. She'd been happy then. Happy to be an owner of her own business. Happy to be away from wait-ressing and more into the business side of things. Happy she had a way to make a good living for a long time.

Even then, though, something had been missing. Sandy felt it as keenly now as she had then. Then, she'd gone home to her dark condo, where she cele-brated with an ice cream cake she'd bought at the grocer. Now, she'd go home to her dark condo—where Tad was staying.

She glanced at him and kept her focus there when he didn't look at her. His striking square jaw and day-old beard called to her. Urged her to touch his face, feel the scruff of his beard as he kissed her.

A flush rose through her like a geyser when he

turned and looked at her. The tether that had been winding between them all day seemed to solidify. He leaned closer. "You ready to go home?"

"Could we?" she asked, glancing at the grandfather clock near the fireplace. "I don't know...my mother might get upset."

"Hank said we could, anytime."

"Isn't he coming?"

"He's going to stay until late," he said. "Doesn't want to leave Willow alone until your parents go to sleep." Tad touched her knee, sending shockwaves down to her foot and up to her head. "Said something about your dad being a night owl."

"He likes to watch the eleven o'clock news," Sandy confirmed. A yawn played with her throat.

"You seem like you're ready to go," Tad said. "And I don't care if we miss dessert."

"We can stop by a drive-through and get ice cream cones," Sandy suggested.

"I like the way you think." Tad tacked a flirty smile to the end of his sentence.

I like you, Sandy thought but didn't say. Still, she struggled with him moving here and taking up a job out at the ranch. Yeah, she knew the job wasn't exactly at Three Rivers Ranch, but he would be driving out there each day, working with horses. It was only a matter of time before he had the boots and the hat and the Texas twang to go with the new job.

He'd asked Brynn a truckload of questions, and then he'd bubbled the whole way back to town about opening a breeding stable. He'd breed the horses; Brynn would train them. It was a win-win, according to Tad.

He'd spent the next hour and a half on the phone with his father, while Sandy helped her mother peel, boil, and whip potatoes into a delectable mash of cheese, salt, sour cream, and butter.

"...not feeling well."

Sandy looked up, surprised to see her mom embracing Tad. "Well, you get on back to Sandy's and lie down."

"I will, ma'am."

She scrambled to her feet when Tad looked at her pointedly. "Thanks for dinner, Mom."

"Tad says he's going to get you two dessert." Her mom smiled at Tad like everything he touched turned to gold. Sandy actually wanted to find out if that was true.

"Ice cream," Tad confirmed. He opened the door and ushered Sandy through it. She'd never been more grateful in her life. When they'd escaped the halo of light from the porch, he slipped his hand into hers.

Sandy ducked her head and tried to hold back her smile.

But she couldn't.

* * *

TAD KEPT Sandy's hand in his for as long as possible. After she'd pulled into her parking lot—and found her spot empty—they strolled toward her condo hand-in-hand. Hank had actually started laughing when Tad had mentioned leaving with Sandy.

He'd sobered quickly enough, though. "You mean you like my sister? Or you *like* my sister?"

"I like her," Tad had said, not giving anything away. "She was nice to me today. Spent her whole day off with me. I just want to thank her." He'd spoken true. He wanted to thank her. Maybe with a kiss.

When Hank had boldly asked him that, Tad had shrugged. "Don't know that she feels the same."

"You be careful with her," Hank warned. "She hasn't had much luck with men."

That hadn't helped Tad's self-conscious worries about being good enough for Sandy. Sandy, who owned a successful and thriving business. Sandy, who seemed to have every aspect of her life together, right down to automatic lights that switched on when she unlocked her front door and entered her condo.

Tad took a deep breath. He hadn't imagined the connection between them, and he wanted to explore it a little bit. Probe. Push. Prod.

He closed the door behind them, his heart suddenly bobbing in the back of his throat. "Too bad everywhere had closed early for Christmas Eve," he said. "We didn't get our ice cream."

"I have lots." Sandy scooted into the kitchen, where she produced a box of ice cream sandwiches, a container of Ben & Jerry's, and a tub of peanut butter cup ice cream. "I have some of that chocolate topping that hardens, if you want that."

"It's fine," he said, grabbing an ice cream sandwich. "I'll have one of these." He nodded toward her balcony. "Anywhere to sit out there?"

"Sure." She put away the ice cream, snagging an ice cream sandwich for herself, and led him onto the balcony.

The breeze cooled Tad's heated skin. The ice cream helped too. The calm, serene countryside before him further calmed him. "Sandy, I'm going to move to Three Rivers."

She sighed, a sad, defeated sound he didn't understand. "I figured."

"I texted my boss while you were making the creamed peas. I quit." He looked at her and found resignation in her expression. "Tell me why that upsets you."

She shrugged and finished her ice cream. She licked her lips, and the desire to do the same exploded through Tad. "Come on." He reached for her hand and brought her knuckles to his lips. "Tell me."

"I had this wild fantasy," she said, her voice small and low. "You know, of you taking me away from Three Rivers in your helicopter. We could fly anywhere, do anything."

He smiled at the wistfulness of her voice, the stunning innocence of her nature, her dazzling beauty. His mind turned, dampening the rising flame in him that kept yelling, *she likes you! She likes you!*

"You don't like Three Rivers?" he asked.

"I like it okay."

"You own the pancake house," he said.

"I know."

Tad frowned, trying to make the pieces align. "Help me understand."

"I bought the pancake house because I...wanted more."

"Will you help me with my breeding stable?"

She shook her head. "I don't know anything about that. Brynn—"

"Has her hands full with her own training business. You could help me with the financials and stuff.

How to deal with a staff, that kind of thing." He squeezed her hand. "Just think about it, will you?"

"I guess."

Frustration boiled through Tad. He'd thought moving here was the right decision—he knew it was. He'd thought Sandy would be happier about it.

"Sandy—"

"Let's go for a walk." She exploded to her feet. "It's not quite dark yet. There's a nice trail around that condo over there. Into a sort of wooded area with a pond."

"Sure." Tad veiled the negative emotions running rampant through him behind a wide smile. "Lead the way."

Thankfully, she pressed her palm to his as she led him through her condo and down the stairs. She turned right and walked behind two more condo buildings before turning right again. Several steps later, the soft glow of muted lamps covered them in golden light. It reflected off the inklings of a stream and soon enough, trees lined the walkway.

"This is beautiful," he said. "So peaceful. That's why I want to move here. I can't feel like this in Vegas."

"It's not always peaceful here," Sandy said.

"Oh, I'm sure." He tugged her a little closer. "Small town. Big rumor mill."

She laughed and finally seemed to relax as she

tucked herself closer to his side. "I'm happy here," she said. "I just sometimes dream of going somewhere else."

"You can travel," he said, barely censoring himself from saying *we*. He liked her. Felt comfortable around her. He wasn't ready to propose marriage or anything crazy like that.

"I don't have time to travel."

"Sure you do," he said. "You took today off."

"It's one day."

"I heard you when I came into the kitchen. You told Gail you wouldn't be in until Tuesday."

"It's Christmas tomorrow." Sandy drifted away and came back. "So it's really just one more day after that. It's no big deal."

Tad stopped walking, his heart thundering in his chest. "Will you take me to church with you tomorrow?" He inched closer and slipped his hands around her waist. A feeling akin to joy flooded him when she leaned into his touch.

"Yes." She slid her hands up his arms, resting them lightly on his shoulders.

"And spend Monday with me? Maybe you can show me all around this little town I'll be living in soon."

"Mm, Monday." She tucked her cheek against his chest, and he thought sure she'd hear the galloping of his heart. He pulled back, hoping she'd tip her head back so he could kiss her.

She did, and the moment between them lengthened. Tad leaned down and pressed his lips to Sandy's. She seemed to sigh against him, seemed to melt into his touch. Encouraged, Tad held on tighter and deepened the kiss.

Chapter Five

Sandy woke on Christmas morning, her eyes snapping open as she remembered the way Tad's lips molded to hers, the gentle way he held her close like she should be cherished, experienced.

She giggled and grinned, the giddy feeling in her gut intensifying as she relived the best kiss of her life. Sighing, she slipped out of bed and into the shower. When she exited her bedroom, fully ready for church, the sky had barely started to lighten.

Her heart dropped. It was only seven o'clock. What was she going to do for the next four hours? Tad surely wouldn't be up and awake this early, and she'd gone to bed before Hank had come in. Her brother had never been one for church anyway, and he'd probably spend Christmas day with his fiancé.

Sandy set the coffee maker to brew and took her

dark roast out to the balcony. She didn't sip the coffee, just let the scent of it wrap around her, curled her fingers around the hot stoneware to keep them warm.

She watched the sunrise paint the landscape before her in beautiful shades of blue and gold. The shadows shortened, finally allowing the sun to take ownership of the day, and Sandy inhaled the possibilities of this day down into her soul.

"I knew I smelled coffee." Tad poked his head out of the now-open French door. "Can I make myself a cup and join you?"

"Yeah," she squeaked. "Yes. Sure."

He grinned, which coated her insides with honey, and ducked back into the condo. He returned a minute later, stirring his brew.

"Can you grab the blanket from the couch?" she asked. "It's chilly out here."

"We can sit inside if you want."

Inside, where it was actually warm. Inside, where Hank could overhear their conversation and maybe see Tad kiss her good morning.

"I'm fine out here. Just need that blanket."

"Sure." Tad set his mug on the tiny table and went to retrieve the blanket. He extended it toward her, and she pulled it. But he didn't let go. She didn't either. She tugged him closer, closer still, until his eyes drifted closed and he kissed her.

"Mm," he said. "You taste like cream."

"You taste like toothpaste."

"Well, I didn't want to share my morning breath." He chuckled and sank into the chair on the other side of the table.

"So you were planning on kissing me, then?"

"Absolutely." He offered her his hand, and she gladly slipped her icy fingers into his, a zip of energy racing along her skin.

She giggled. "Don't let Hank hear you say that."

"I already cleared things with Hank."

Sandy almost choked on her drink. "You did what?"

"I told him I liked you." He spoke so matter-of-factly, like any man would like her, want to date her.

And fine, yes. Sandy knew she was pretty, and plenty of men asked her out. It was maintaining that interest she couldn't seem to accomplish. Sudden fear gripped her heart and squeezed. Had she kissed Tad too early? Shown her attraction to him too soon? She folded into herself and tucked the blanket around her tighter, trying not to lose herself to the worries. Tad was still here, after all.

They passed the hours with easy conversation, most of it revolving around Hank as a child and then Tad detailing his ideas for a boarding and breeding stable. When Sandy walked into church on Tad's arm, no one so much as looked her way.

The gossips were used to Sandy showing up on the arm of a handsome man. Her friends encouraged her many and varied relationships. Usually.

Andy Larsen, the boutique owner, caught her eye and raised her eyebrows. A moment later, Sandy's phone vibrated in her jacket pocket. She knew who it was from and what Andy wanted to know.

Sandy loved Andy; they'd grown up together in Three Rivers and now each owned a small business in the heart of the town. She tapped out a reply. *Tad Jorgensen. Hank's friend from college. Former helicopter pilot.*

She frowned at the last part of the text, then erased it. She managed to press send before the organ began playing and she stuffed her phone back into her pocket. Tad's arm rested lightly across her back, the weight of it borne by the pew. His hand draped lazily down her shoulder, and she nestled a bit closer to him.

He smiled down at her before focusing back on the pulpit. The scent of him after a shower—all piney and minty and spicy—kept teasing Sandy's nose and urging her to just get a tiny bit closer.

She managed to squash the wicked thought—she was in church, after all—and listen to what Pastor Scott had to say.

"Every decision is important," he said. "But don't spend so much time worryin' about what to do that you don't actually do anything."

Sandy agreed. She'd had some experience there. The pancake house had been up for sale for six months —and survived two failed attempts to buy it—before she made the decision and came up with the cash.

"Some decisions allow future opportunities. And some will close some doors we don't even know about yet. Know where you want to go, and make the decisions that will get you there."

Sandy wondered if she was making the right choices. If she wanted to leave Three Rivers, she wasn't. Tad's arm suddenly weighed ten times more than it had a few seconds ago. If she followed the path with him, she'd never leave town.

You can travel, he'd said to her once.

And he was right.

She didn't really want to leave Three Rivers. If she had, she wouldn't have chosen to buy the pancake house. Or her condo.

Satisfied that she could live a happy life in Three Rivers, she stood and joined in singing the last hymn. Tad stayed in his seat, but she could feel his eyes trained on her. Glancing at him, she noticed he didn't sing at all.

She bent down. "You don't sing?"

"Nobody wants to hear me sing."

Sandy reached for his hands and pulled him up. "I do."

"No, Sandy, really."

"Come on." She gave him her best smile. "It's Christmas."

He returned it with a tight-lipped smile that didn't reach his eyes. He opened his mouth, but he didn't sing. Instead, he mouthed the words, ignoring her when she protested. The song ended, and he sat back down, pulling her close as she settled into place beside him.

"I want to hear you sing," she whispered.

"Maybe later."

Later didn't come during the rest of the service as the choir took over with songs about the Savior's birth. When they returned to her condo, they found it empty. A note sat on the counter: *Gone to mom's. Be back late again.*

"So Hank's out," she said, tossing the note in the trash. "I told you I don't actually cook. Everywhere will be closed for Christmas. But I have some stuff we can probably make into something edible. You game?"

A mischievous twinkle entered his eye. "So it's just me and you, all day, alone?" He came around the peninsula and crowded into the kitchen. "What a great Christmas gift."

"Tad," she warned.

"What?" He slid his hands around her waist and traced his lips along her neck. "I just want to kiss you again."

Sandy had a hard time keeping herself upright, what with the fireworks popping in her bloodstream. "One kiss. Then we figure out the food situation. I'm starving."

"One kiss," he murmured moments before he touched his mouth to hers.

Time could've dripped away. Or fallen like a raging river down a mountainside. Sandy had no idea if he'd kissed her once or a hundred times by the time he pulled away. All she knew was that she was falling hard, and fast, and though she should be screaming and searching for a handhold, she really wanted to take another leap.

* * *

MONDAY MORNING FOUND her at the pancake house ten minutes before it opened. The coffee was hot. The grills steaming. The wait staff and hostess standing by. Sandy sat at her favored table with Gail. They'd exchanged hellos and spoken of the restaurant for a few minutes. Nothing had been said about Tad, though Sandy's mind circled him constantly.

"So I'll be out the rest of the week," Sandy finally said. "You sure you'll be okay?"

"Absolutely sure," Gail said, the same way she had the previous three times. She stood and collected the coffee cups from the table. "Go have fun with your new man."

"He's not my new man," Sandy said, the idea sending cold fear through her veins. "He's just an old friend. We're getting to know each other again."

"I'll bet." Gail smiled and took the mugs into the kitchen. Sighing, but satisfied with her decision—and what doors it could open for her—Sandy headed home. She expected Tad might be awake, but the light in his bedroom remained off.

She entered the condo thinking she might slip back to bed for a couple of hours. But Hank sat on the couch facing the front door. Arms crossed, eyebrows drawn, he watched her enter and close the door.

"You're up early," she said, kicking off her shoes and shrugging out of her jacket.

"I wanted to talk to you."

She curled herself into the couch. "All right. What's up?"

"Tell me about Tad."

Sandy groaned and got up. She headed into the kitchen to make more coffee. This conversation definitely required copious amounts of liquid caffeine. "I thought you were going to ask me if I liked Willow or something."

"This is more important."

"It is?" She practically slammed the lid to her coffee maker, and she winced. The machine cost too much to treat so poorly. "She's going to be my sister-in-law. The only other woman. I'll have to go on, like, girls' trips with her and stuff."

Hank grunted. "So do you like her?"

"Besides, you already know Tad. You guys get along great. There's no issue there."

"What are you saying?"

"I'm not saying anything." She added milk to her coffee and blew on it to cool it down.

"Are you guys dating?"

"I don't know. We...hang out. Talk. It's nice."

"You hang out and talk." He sounded like she'd just told him she and Tad had started a knitting club together.

"Yes, Hank, we hang out and talk. I don't appreciate your tone."

"My tone?" He stood and faced her. "Look, I know what 'hang out and talk' means to a man. There's more to it than that."

"Is there?" Sandy sipped her coffee. "I wouldn't know. I'm not a man."

Hank growled. "You know what I mean."

"I'm sure I don't." Sandy glared at her brother. Why was he being so overprotective? He'd never cared who she dated before. Never.

She'd also never tried to date one of his friends.

"I don't want you to get hurt."

"I'm an adult," Sandy reminded him. "And I know what I'm doing." In fact, she was making conscious decisions about her life. "But I would like to know what 'hang out and talk' means to a man...."

A smile cracked Hank's stony exterior. "He told me he liked you."

"He told me the same thing." The heat in Sandy's face could've come from the coffee. But she knew it didn't. It came because she liked Tad too. Maybe more than she should. Maybe more than was smart.

"You like him too?"

"Yes."

"Did he kiss you?"

"I don't have to answer that."

"Oh, okay. He did." Hank ran his hands through his hair.

"I don't know why you're freaking out about this." Concern spiked in Sandy. What about Tad had Hank worried? Should Sandy be worried too?

"He lives in Las Vegas," Hank said. "You own a pancake house in Three Rivers."

Confusion needled Sandy. "He's moving here, Hank. He quit his job in Vegas."

"He what?"

Sandy backpedaled, trying to think of what to say next. Tad obviously hadn't been as forthcoming with Hank regarding his life plans and decisions. She didn't want to be the one to tell his private matters.

"You'll have to ask him about it." Sandy side-stepped her brother. "I'm going back to bed for a while."

"Me too." Hank stomped in the other direction, slamming the door behind him. Sandy shook her head as she returned, much quieter, to her bedroom. Tad had said he'd spoken to Hank about her, about *them*.

So what was Hank's problem?

Or did the problem belong to Sandy? She retreated to the mirror, searching, searching, searching for that fatal flaw that would end things with Tad, the way it had ended every other relationship.

She couldn't find it. Frustrated, she fell back into bed, a prayer on her lips that she could find the flaw and rip it out of herself. *Just this once*, she begged. *Please, Lord, just this once, let me be enough for someone.*

* * *

Tad didn't see Sandy or Hank when he emerged from the office where he slept. He'd planned to borrow Hank's truck and spend the morning at the ranch, walking through Brynn's facilities and drawing up plans to add on a boarding stable. He'd scheduled to meet with the owner of Three Rivers Ranch, as well as the founder of Courage Reins, an equine therapy program housed at the ranch.

Tad thought he might be able to use existing buildings for his breeding program, and he wanted advice from everyone willing to give it.

He helped himself to Sandy's coffee supply, marveling at her one-cup-at-a-time machine and thinking he needed to invest in such a thing. He doctored his drink up with cream and sugar and turned. A box on the kitchen table caught his attention, especially because his name adorned the envelope leaning against it.

Tad set down his mug and reached for the box. He suspected it was a cowboy hat, and a smile tugged at the corners of his mouth. After opening the card, he found Sandy's handwriting.

A cowboy needs a hat. ~Sandy

He took out the dark brown hat, holding it gently by the crown. This was no cheap knockoff. This was pure fur felt, and Tad settled it on his head. The hat felt like it belonged there, and he wondered how he'd managed to walk around Texas for the past few days without it in place.

He'd noticed the cowboys here never took their hats off, not even for church. And now he knew why. He strode into the living room, where Sandy had a mirror hung on the wall. Tad admired the craftsmanship of the hat, the way it made him seem more mysterious, less open to scrutiny.

His pulse sped as he turned toward Sandy's bedroom door. He wanted to thank her. He glanced at his hands like the perfect gift would appear and he could present her with it. He couldn't even think of what she'd like.

Guilt tore through him with the power of a freight train. Here he was, kissing his best friend's sister, and he didn't even know what she'd like for a gift.

He couldn't swallow. Air seemed like the wrong thing to breathe. Disbelief at his behavior made him doubt how he'd felt about Sandy. How he felt about moving to Three Rivers. How he felt about everything he'd done since arriving four days ago.

Leaving his coffee to cool on the table, he scrambled back to the office to grab his wallet and Hank's keys, and then he got out of Sandy's condo before he had to face her.

He wasn't even sure why he didn't want to see her. Shouldn't he want to express his gratitude?

"That's why," he muttered to himself as he hurried toward Hank's truck. He *did* want to express his gratitude—with a kiss. Lots of kisses. The truck roared to life, drowning out his guilty thoughts.

The clear blue sky calmed him, pushed out some of the guilt at what he'd done, what he still wanted to do.

So he liked Sandy, and she just happened to be Hank's sister. Was that so wrong?

He'd even talked to Hank about a relationship with Sandy. Tad didn't know how to feel. Confused? Frustrated? Guilty?

Making a quick decision, he pulled to the side of the road and swiped on his phone. *Are you awake?* he sent to Sandy.

When she didn't answer, he made another choice. He swung around and headed back to her condo. He marched up the stairs and back into the living room right as his phone sounded.

Sandy's name popped up. *Yeah, coming out.*

Her bedroom door opened a moment later, and Sandy stood there, wearing a pink and white plaid sundress with a white sweater covering her shoulders. Her smile made his heart patter harder, and he threw every plaguing worry out the window.

"Thanks for the hat."

"It looks nice on you." She took a step closer,

moving close enough to reach out and touch the brim. "Very handsome."

"You didn't need to buy me a hat."

She fell back as if he'd struck her and ducked her head. "You don't like it?"

"I like it fine."

"I thought I heard someone leave already."

"Yeah, that was me. Now I'm going to be late getting out to the ranch."

She fixed him with a cold glare that lasted for one, two breaths before she looked away. "Well, I won't keep you."

Tad didn't know what to say. The words inside his brain wouldn't order themselves to come out his mouth the right way.

"You can go," she said. "And you don't have to wear the hat if you don't want to." Sandy stepped toward her bedroom.

"Why wouldn't—?" he started, but the door closed before he could finish. He didn't understand what had just happened. He'd come back to tell her thanks, show her he cared about her and not just about kissing her. What had he said wrong?

Familiar insecurity bloomed inside him. He couldn't handle a machine, make it do what he wanted. What made him think he could tame a woman? Especially one as beautiful and successful as Sandy.

She doesn't want you, a voice whispered in his head. The same one that hissed things like, *You almost let that family die. You shouldn't fly anymore.*

He tried to push out the poisonous voice, but it only seemed to get louder. By the time he arrived at Three Rivers Ranch, Tad was sure every person he met would be able to read his failures as if they were printed on his forehead.

Pete Marshall and Squire Ackerman stood near the edge of the barn, engaged in deep conversation with Brynn Bowman. A part of Tad died with every second that passed. Though his presentation had gone well, his walk-through had been thorough, and he'd managed to obliterate his insecurities before he came face-to-face with anyone, the serious set of Squire's mouth didn't look promising.

Pete had been more open to Tad's business proposal. He'd even said, "And any horses that you can't train, Brynn, or that you can't sell, Tad, we could absorb into Courage Reins."

Tad had been impressed with the equine therapy program Pete ran. It seemed to operate without a hitch, and their facilities were top-notch. Every cowhand could answer any of Tad's questions, and after spending an hour with Pete, he knew why his men obeyed him.

Tad's biggest opponent turned out to be Garth Ahlstrom, the foreman at the ranch, who'd followed him around wearing a look the color of a winter storm. And he'd put a bug in Squire's ear. Something about having more people out on the ranch, more buildings, less land, more distractions, less peace.

Tad wasn't sure how any more peace could possibly exist out here. Every cell in his body found joy in the whispering breeze, the gentle sound of horses nickering and cattle lowing. The smell of straw and chickens and someone slow roasting meat reminded him of home, of happier times, of the kind of life he craved.

And his anxiety skyrocketed again. His muscles would surely snap from the constant tension. His teeth certainly ached.

Finally, Squire glanced his way, and Tad found the softening he'd hoped for. Squire nodded, and Pete turned toward Tad. The men came forward as a single unit, and Tad wondered at their history, at what could create such unity between them, even when they clearly disagreed. Brynn trailed in their wake, and Tad remembered that she'd just moved to town recently.

"We'd love to have you out at Three Rivers," Pete

said, extending his hand for Tad to shake. "Isn't that right, Major?"

"Yeah," Squire said, spearing Pete with a look that said otherwise. "But we can't build any more buildings. My foreman says he'll quit if I allow more construction, and I can't lose him."

"More like you can't lose Juliette's cinnamon rolls on Sunday morning." Pete grinned at Squire and then Tad. "I'll save you one. They're amazing."

Squire grunted. "So Brynn's agreed to rent you stable space for your boarding program. She'll really only have a few horses here at a time as she trains them."

Tad nodded at Brynn, hoping his smile and eyes conveyed his gratitude.

"There should be plenty of room," Brynn said, offering him a friendly smile.

"And Pete's gonna let you use his barn for breeding. Brynn has contacts in that field, as does Pete. You can use his indoor arena if you need to." He glanced at Pete and Brynn. "Did I cover it all?"

"You'll have to live in town and commute," Pete said. "Squire's cowboy cabins are full."

"No problem," Tad said, thinking of enlisting Sandy's help to find somewhere to live. "I won't be ready to start until after the New Year anyway. Even then, it'll be slow at first."

"Not as slow as you think," Brynn said. "I had two guys contact me this morning about boarding. I told them you'd call them back this afternoon." She extracted a piece of paper from her pocket and gave it to him. "So I'd call them back this afternoon."

"And those calls are what pushed Squire over the edge," Pete added. "So be nice to them." He clapped Tad on the shoulder. "I'm glad to have you. My granddaddy had a boarding stable, and I loved going there."

Sudden emotion gripped Tad's throat, so he nodded and managed to squeeze out a "Thank you," before the trio stepped away to continue their work.

His only thought was to get back to Sandy and share his good news. With every mile he drove, though, his excitement fizzled. Would she be happy for him? She'd argued with him considerably when he'd spoken of quitting flying, of moving here and opening a boarding stable.

But then she'd given him the cowboy hat.

Tad couldn't make sense of her actions, but he really wanted to. Before, he might have let her pull back, hide in her bedroom, and then drift away from him completely. He'd never needed a woman in his life, at least not for long. But since the incident where he'd barely made it back to safety, he yearned to have someone to come home to. Someone to share his innermost feelings with. Someone to trust and confide in.

Coming home to his empty apartment had added to his anxiety, and he often found himself going out to eat and staying until the restaurant closed, just so he didn't have to be truly alone.

"I don't want to be alone anymore," he said out loud to make it stick. He just hoped he could find the right words to say to Sandy.

Chapter Six

S andy paced in her kitchen, the peace offering she'd made sitting on the counter, mocking her. She reached for a cookie and practically stuffed the whole thing in her mouth. Tad should be getting back any minute. She had spies out at the ranch, and Chelsea had texted forty-five minutes ago.

He just left.

So he should be back any minute.

Any minute.

Plagued by her conversation with Hank, and worried that her gift had been given too soon, she'd retreated that morning, unwilling to have a hard conversation or allow herself to get hurt.

Truth was, she expected to be hurt. To be broken up with. To be kissed and then abandoned. And while she'd known Tad for a few years now, before this week-end, they'd been nothing more than acquaintances. She had no idea how he normally treated women, or if he'd had long-term relationships, or anything.

What she did know scared her. She knew she'd started to fall for him, only four days in. She knew she pictured him by her side next Christmas. She knew she thought of him constantly and—

"Hey."

She spun at the sound of his voice, surprised she'd let her thoughts run so rampant that she hadn't heard him enter her condo.

"More cookies?" he asked, eyeing them with appreciation.

"I'm sorry about this morning." She picked up a cookie and thrust it toward him.

He took it and bit into it, his eyes drifting closed for a moment. "You'll notice I wore the hat all day."

"It looks good on you." She wrapped her arms around herself as if cold, but the smoldering look he gave her warmed her from top to bottom.

"Thank you." He finished his cookie and moved into her personal space. "I'm sorry about this morning too. I wasn't sure of the protocol. And I didn't have a gift for you, and I was worried about how things would go at the ranch, and...." He took her in his arms. "I've been wantin' to kiss you all day to say thank you."

"That's not necessary." Sandy enjoyed the heat of

his hands on her back, the delicious scent of fresh air and chocolate that surrounded him.

"Kissing you isn't necessary?" He grinned. "I think you're totally wrong about that. I'm dying a slow death here." He leaned down to kiss her, but the brim of his hat bumped into her forehead.

"Hat," she said, giggling.

He took the hat off and set it on the table. "I need more practice, obviously."

"I'd prefer you don't kiss anyone else." Sandy ran her fingers through his somewhat matted hair.

"Wasn't planning to." He leaned down and touched his lips to hers, hesitant at first. Sandy knew they had a lot more to talk about—including his future at the ranch—but for now, she just wanted to enjoy kissing him.

So she did.

$$* * *$$

"Turn left up there," Sandy directed. They'd escaped Three Rivers to go to dinner, and Tad drove her car into Wellington and turned left.

"Oh, I see it."

The diner ahead on the left wasn't hard to spot. With only a movie theater and a dark office building to make up downtown Wellington, Sandy suddenly appreciated the bustle of downtown Three Rivers.

She pulled out her phone and texted Andy, who had sent a message a few hours earlier, inviting Sandy over for dinner at her loft. And though Sandy loved her friend and normally would've gone, Andy had just gotten back together with her boyfriend, Lawrence, and Sandy didn't enjoy feeling like a third wheel.

Bring Tad, Andy had said.

Sorry, Sandy texted now. *We decided to go to dinner in Wellington. Rain check?*

She sent the messages as Tad flipped a U-turn and parked in front of the diner. "I gotta say, this place doesn't look open."

"It is," Sandy said. "It's just Monday night, so it's not going to be busy or anything."

He shifted toward her. "Is Monday usually slow?"

"Tuesday night is the slowest night for me," she said. "It's why we have family specials, kids eat free, that kind of thing." She grinned at him, glad everything between them felt so comfortable. "Let's go eat."

They became the second table in the diner, and Sandy settled into a booth with Tad across from her. "So tell me how things went at the ranch." Though the thought of him becoming a full-fledged cowboy made her heart fill with cement, she wanted him to be happy.

"It's going to work out," he said. "I won't have my

own facilities, but I'm going to rent stable space from Brynn and partner with the ranch and Courage Reins to use their barns and arenas." Excitement sparked in his voice and brightened his eyes, causing a smile to pull at Sandy's lips.

He continued to speak about all the things he needed to line up before he could really start, but he was planning to spend most of tomorrow talking to his father, who owned a boarding stable in Wyoming.

Sandy nodded and smiled and "mm-hmm"'ed in all the right places. She ate her anxiety away with a cheeseburger and sweet potato fries, unable to identify why Tad's new career made her skin seem like someone had turned it inside out.

"You seem happier," she finally said.

"I feel happier." Tad wiped his fingers on a napkin and set it down. "Just knowing I don't have to go back to Vegas is a huge relief."

"How will you get all your stuff here?" Sandy leaned her elbows on the table and tried to see his eyes under that blasted cowboy hat. As much as it increased his good looks, she'd forgotten that she hated not being able to see a man's eyes when he wore a cowboy hat.

"I'll hire someone," he said. "I'm not going back."

She cocked her head and gave him a teasing smile. "So you're going to live out of my office?"

He reached across the table and took her hands in

his. "Yeah, that has to change, even if I like being so close to you." He ducked his head as a smile enhanced his handsomeness. "Will you help me find somewhere to rent? I can look to buy something later."

Curiosity burned through Sandy. How much money did Tad have? If he could afford to hire someone to pack up his life in Vegas and move it Three Rivers, he certainly had enough to buy something now.

"I'm lookin' to go cheap for now," he said, and the cowboy twang in his speech sent a spike of annoyance through Sandy. She couldn't believe she was on a date with another cowboy!

"Oh?" she said. "Maybe you should get back to Vegas and pack yourself. Save some money." She didn't mean for her tone to be quite so sharp.

Tad watched her, the light in his eyes now more cautious than flirty. "I have an appointment with the loan manager at the bank on Wednesday. Though I don't have any construction costs, I'm going to need to pay Brynn rent, and I need supplies, and funds to pay stud fees." His face reddened, and Sandy wasn't sure if it was from talk about stud fees or because he needed money to start his business.

"But I'm not goin' back to Vegas. I have a severance package I can use to pay for the move and for a cheap apartment." His voice darkened with every word. By the time he finished, Sandy's annoyance had faded and regret had taken its place.

She sighed. "I'm sorry."

"It's fine." He graced her with a quick grin that didn't hold the luster it sometimes did. "You still hung up on me whisking you away from Three Rivers?" The teasing quality of his words told her he wasn't upset.

"Yeah, something like that," she said.

"And this wasn't good enough?" He gestured to the haphazard décor of the diner. "I'm shocked by that."

Sandy laughed along with Tad, the release a welcome change. She needed to get over her fantasy of leaving Three Rivers and living an exotic life on a white-sand beach. It wasn't the life she wanted anyway.

"This was fun," she said as he threw some cash on the table and stood.

"Good." He slid his arm around her waist. "When I'm with you, I don't much care where I am."

Warmth and peace infused Sandy's dark and cold areas. She didn't need to leave Three Rivers to be happy. Maybe Tad moving to town would be exactly what she needed. She snuggled into his side, afraid to speak of such long-term things so soon into their relationship.

Hank's salty attitude toward Tad kissing her revolved through her mind. She needed to ask Tad about Hank, about why her brother wouldn't want them to be together. But after Tad's declaration that he just liked being with her, she decided to clamp her lips shut and save her questions for another day.

She reached for the radio and turned up the volume. "Okay, let's hear your singing voice."

He gave her an incredulous look. "Yeah, right."

"Come on," she begged, glad for the excuse for lighter conversation. "I want to hear you sing."

His grip tightened on the steering wheel. "Okay, but I'm terrible."

"Can't be that bad."

He opened his mouth and sang the next line in the chorus. Sandy gaped at him, sure what was coming from his mouth wasn't even English. She burst out laughing, and he cut off the noise.

"See?" He hunched down in the seat, pulling his cowboy hat lower and hiding under it. "You don't have to laugh so hard."

"I thought you were kidding."

"I rarely joke about my flaws."

Sandy reached over and took his hand in hers. "I thought it was...special." But secretly, she was glad Tad had flaws. They made her more comfortable about him, made him more human, and though she still thought him to be nearly perfect, she could always fall back on his terrible singing when her ideals about him grew too large.

He lifted her fingers to his mouth and kissed them. "So no more singing?"

"No," she said. "We'll leave that to the professionals."

By Tuesday evening, Tad's brain felt like it had been taken out of his skull, run over and bruised, and then reinserted. He'd spent most of the day in Sandy's office, his own notes now littering the desk.

His father had been more than generous, giving him advice and emailing him a list of supplies to start his boarding program. He'd called the two men Brynn had referred him to regarding breeding and they were coming on Monday.

Monday!

Tad groaned and rubbed the kink out of the back of his neck. He could be ready by Saturday. He'd have to be.

While he'd only planned to stay in town for several days, everything had changed once he'd actually arrived. He still hadn't done anything about his apartment in Las Vegas, but the thought of making another phone call made a stabbing pain materialize behind his eyes.

Tomorrow, he told himself as he emerged from the office. Sandy's living room and kitchen sat empty. Not surprising, since darkness loomed beyond the windows as well. She'd probably gone out to eat, Tad thought, as his own stomach roared.

His phone rang, and he wanted to flush it down the toilet. Though it had been a good day, full of needed information, he didn't want to talk to anyone else.

"Hey, Sandy," he said, trying to make his voice brighter than he felt.

"Are you coming to my mom's for dinner? We're waiting."

A rush of adrenaline seemed to wake his brain. She'd left her car for him and gone with Hank earlier that day. She'd spent hours with Willow, and she hadn't been looking forward to it. And now he was late.

"Yeah," he said. "I'm on my way now. Sorry I'm running a bit behind. Go ahead and start without me."

She sighed. "You don't sound like you're driving." Her lowered voice could only mean she'd called him right from the dinner table. He didn't want to embarrass her in front of her family. In fact, she'd told him on the way home from Wellington last night that she felt like she didn't fit in her family. He'd wanted to provide a refuge for her, a place she did belong. He still did, and he mentally kicked himself for losing track of time, for forgetting Sandy needed him.

"I'm on my way out the door." He searched for his shoes, wishing he had time to change and make himself more presentable for her family.

"Okay, well, get here fast."

He promised he would and then hung up. He grabbed her keys from the counter, slid on his athletic shoes, and flew out the door. He shouldn't have to doctor himself up for dinner at his best friend's house. But for his *girlfriend's* parents....

Tad didn't quite know how to act anymore. He'd eaten and slept at Hank's many times. But he hadn't eaten and slept at Sandy's. The territory suddenly felt a lot more treacherous.

Thankfully, he made it across town in record time, and they'd started without him. He slid into a seat next to Sandy, wanting to lean over and press a kiss to her temple, maybe murmur a heartfelt apology.

Instead, he smiled at her mom and apologized for being late. She grinned at him and handed him a bowl of mashed potatoes. Dinner passed, and Tad noticed Sandy's suffering.

She finally stood. "Well, I'm going into work early tomorrow. So I'm gonna head out."

Her going to work was news to Tad. She'd taken the whole week off—or so he'd thought. Hank apparently thought the same thing, because he pierced her with a glare and then switched his murderous look to Tad.

Tad shrugged and followed Sandy out into the night. "I'm real sorry I was late." He didn't dare touch her—he could barely keep up with her. "What happened in there?"

She marched to the driver's side of her car and held out her palm. "Keys, please."

"I'll drive."

"I'd rather drive."

Tad stopped a few feet away from her and tried to figure out what he'd done wrong. "Sandy, I—"

"I just want the keys."

Determination filled Tad. He lifted his chin. "No." He tucked the keys in his jacket pocket. "Tell me what happened in there."

She met his eyes, and though it was mostly dark, a light from the porch illuminated the fear and anger in her expression. "Were you ever going to tell me about Sarah?"

His heart hammered a couple times before sinking to his shoes. Hank. The scowl made sense now. "Of course," Tad said. "We haven't talked about past relationships yet." It was a painful reminder that he'd been in town for five days, that this relationship wasn't even a week old yet. "That's usually several dates in." He dared to take a step closer. "What did Hank say?"

"That you were engaged."

"True."

"That she was pregnant, and when she lost the baby, she broke things off."

Shame and regret filled Tad. "Also true." He took a deep breath. "And I'm not the same person I was back then. Did he tell you this was years and years ago?"

Sandy nodded. "He did mention it happened right after you first moved to Vegas."

"I'm different now."

"He also said that you haven't really seen the need to have anyone in your life since."

He swallowed. "Mostly true."

"Who?" she asked.

"Just God."

She seemed to deflate with those words, and Tad stepped into her personal space and gathered her into his arms. "Until you, Sandy. Until you."

She relaxed into his embrace, and Tad felt the tiniest bit bad about saying such things. He'd been fine alone until the accident. But since then, even God hadn't been able to soothe him. Nothing had. No one could.

Until her.

So he had spoken the truth, maybe just not all of it.

"Let me tell you about it," he said as he unlocked the car and escorted her around to the passenger side. As he moved back to get into the driver's seat, he prayed for courage and strength.

And for Sandy to have an understanding heart. Because if she didn't, he'd find himself on the streets of Three Rivers alone tomorrow, looking for an apartment without the help of the woman he felt himself falling for.

Chapter Seven

Sandy woke on Wednesday morning to the sound of knocking. Several moments passed before she realized the noise came from her bedroom door. Flinging off the nightmares of her slumber the same way she did her comforter, she jumped out of bed and hurried to the door.

Tad stood on the other side, his handsome face bearing the lines of exhaustion. He painted over them with a smile. "Hey, gorgeous." He hugged her and retreated a few steps. "I thought we were going apartment shopping this morning."

The fact that he hadn't left in the dead of night, that he still wanted to spend time with her, testified of his gentle soul and calm strength. After all, she'd practically poured out every one of her insecurities to him last night as they discussed his past relationships—and hers.

He waited, his watchful eyes refusing to look anywhere but at her. She noticed the slant of the sunlight as it poured through the sliding glass doors in the kitchen. "What time is it?"

"Almost noon."

"Tad, I'm sorry." She ran her hand through her hair, panic welling where her pulse should be.

"Don't." He stepped into her and took her hand in his as it fell back to her side. "I wanted you to sleep. We were up way too late last night."

She didn't try to mask the raw fear, the naked need, in her expression when she looked at him. "Did you get any sleep?"

"A little." He smiled, and she lost herself in his charms, his exquisite patience, his solid strength holding her up. "I heard you sawing logs this morning, so I know you did."

She playfully pushed against his chest, a giggle in her throat. "Let me shower, and we'll go. I printed some listings."

He released her and gestured toward the dining room table. "I got them. I'll make you some coffee too."

She grinned in response and closed the door between them. Leaning against it, she offered a prayer of gratitude that Tad hadn't left. She was so used to the men in her life doing so, she didn't quite know what to do with one who didn't.

Love him, came into her mind, and she startled away from the door lest he could hear her thoughts. Still, giddiness swept through her. Could she love Tad Jorgensen?

And even better, could he love her in return?

As she hurried into the bathroom to look at herself in the mirror, she finally saw a woman who could be loved.

She's always been there. The thought came from somewhere outside of Sandy, but she knew it to be true. Tears welled in her eyes. "Maybe I just needed to wait for the right man to come to town."

She didn't wait for confirmation from herself or from the Lord. She turned and got in the shower, at peace in Three Rivers for the first time in her life.

* * *

"I LIKED that second one the best." Sandy sighed as she collapsed on a park bench. They'd been apartment hunting for the better part of five hours, and her feet ached. Though she spent a large part of each day walking and standing at work, the emotional toll of finding Tad a place to live weighed much heavier than getting cakes out to table three.

"Me too." Tad sat next to her and handed her an all-meat calzone. The sun flirted with the horizon as they ate. With darkness falling and winter winds blowing, the park remained deserted except for them.

"I want you to meet my parents," Tad said. He spoke so quietly, Sandy wasn't sure his whispered words weren't part of the wind.

She turned toward him as if encased in quicksand, questions stuck in her throat.

He didn't look at her, but studied his hands. "I'm falling in love with you, and I want to take you to Stillwater to meet my parents." He lifted his head and met her gaze. The penetrating emotion in his dark-diamond eyes amplified what he'd said.

"You're falling in love with me?"

Her first thought was *impossible.*

Her second was *I'm falling in love with him too.*

"More every day." He reached for her hand and dropped his eyes back to the ground. "And I know I've been in town for five days, and it's fast and all that. I'm not asking you to marry me. But I feel good about us. I feel the same way about you that I felt about moving here, about starting the boarding stable. And." He sighed. "I don't know. I need to go home for a few days anyway, and I thought maybe you'd like to come."

"Of course." The words exploded from her mouth.

"Of course I want to meet your parents. I want to see the town where you grew up."

Their eyes locked again, and he emitted a nervous chuckle at the same time she released a shaky laugh.

"Okay, then," he said. "We can go tomorrow. I have to be back on Monday for those two boarders, and I'll need a day or so to get the space at Brynn's ready."

"Tomorrow," Sandy echoed, a sense of wonder floating through her. She actually craved what tomorrow would hold for her, and she'd never felt like that before.

* * *

TAD FELT like a long-tailed cat in a room full of rocking chairs. The flight to Wyoming had only taken a couple of hours, and his mother and father had agreed to pick him up at the airport. He hadn't told them about bringing home Sandy. He figured his mother's questions wouldn't have as much time to accumulate that way.

Plus, he hadn't brought a woman home in well, he'd never brought a woman home. Not even Sarah, when she was going to have his child. They hadn't made it that far before she lost the baby and ran away.

After that, Tad had doubted if she was pregnant at all, though he'd never told anyone that. No sense in talking bad about the woman, and her departure had made him realize how unprepared he was to be a father, to be married. How stupid his actions had been. Eight years had passed since then, and he'd been flying helicopters and going to church. Both had fulfilled him, until the near-accident.

"Is that her?" Sandy's cool voice brought him out of his memories. He looked up to find his mom waving madly from near the baggage claim.

"That's her." He tugged on Sandy's hand to get her to pause. "I didn't exactly tell her you were coming."

She blinked at him, the shock in her eyes not exactly comforting. Her fingers released his. "Why didn't you tell her I was coming with you? I thought that was the whole point of giving me less than twelve hours to tie things up with my busy pancake house and pack my bag and get to the airport." She fell back a step and it felt like a mile to Tad. "I thought you wanted me to meet them."

"I did; I do."

"But you didn't tell them I was coming." She cocked her hip and folded her arms. Tad wished he didn't find her so adorable when she was angry.

"I—"

"C'mon, cowboy." Her tone could've melted metal. "Let's go meet them."

Tad blinked as she stormed away from him, as a

squeal erupted from her mouth, as she engulfed his petite mother in a friendly hug. His father stared at the exchange and then switched his eagle eye to Tad. The bewilderment spurred Tad to cross the distance between them and give his dad a quick hug and pat on the back.

Sandy stepped back from his mom, brushing against his side. She slid her hand into his, a movement Tad felt like everyone in the Casper airport catalogued. His mother certainly did.

"Mom." Tad's voice caught against itself. He hadn't seen her in a long time, but he knew the emotion spiraling through his body had more to do with Sandy than with his long absence from Wyoming.

"This is Sandy Keller," he said, glancing at her. The warm smile that came so easily to his face appeared. "You remember my college roommate, Hank Keller? This is his sister."

His mother seemed to have lost her ability to speak, and his dad never had said much. Tad's mouth dried out as the seconds passed.

"Tad wanted me to come meet y'all," Sandy said. "We just have our carry-ons, so we can head to the car."

That got his dad's feet moving, and Tad thanked the stars that Sandy had experience chatting with strangers. She asked his mother about her house, the boarding stable, Tad's siblings, the horses. With her questions and his mother's answers, Tad didn't have to speak until they pulled into Stillwater.

"Tell me about the town, Tad," Sandy said, increasing the pressure on his fingers, which he hadn't let go of once during the hour-long drive from the airport.

"It's pretty in the summer," he said. "The snow makes everything seem dead and deserted." Tad had always hated Stillwater in the winter, which had prompted him to leave town only a few days after his high school graduation.

"The snow is pretty," Sandy said. "You know, I've never actually seen it."

"You've never seen snow?" Tad swung his attention to her. "Well, now I feel like I should've made a bigger deal of it when we came out of the airport." It certainly had blown in his face like it had a personal vendetta against him.

"This is downtown," his father said, turning down Main Street. Tad saw familiar shops—the local deli where his high school crush used to work, the movie theater where he'd sneak up to the balcony even when it was closed, the barber shop where his dad probably still got his hair cut.

Newer additions lined the streets too—a cell phone store, and a fast food restaurant he'd enjoyed in Vegas, and a place where kids could go to jump on trampolines. The street surrounding that establishment was particularly packed.

"This is cute," Sandy said. "I can't believe you didn't like this place."

His mother made a soft huffing sound that Tad chose to ignore. "Snow," he said instead. "Can you imagine driving to work the morning after you get two feet of snow?"

"It can't be that bad."

"Sometimes we don't leave the house for days," he said. "Because it *is* that bad."

She stared at him, horrified. "He's lying, right, Brian?"

"He's not." Tad's father turned to head out to the house.

"We live on the edge of town," Tad said. "Literally. Like right on the border of Stillwater. Most of the boarding stable is technically part of the county, not the township." He did love the drive out to the house. He used to ride his bike down the street, pumping hard to get to town to meet his friends. He'd curse the miles, but when he got home and didn't have to deal with anything but crickets and the wide open sky, he did like it.

The miles went by quickly, and soon enough, his dad pulled down the driveway of the ranch home. "Okay, here we are." A hill of ants crowded into his stomach, and he wasn't even sure why. Probably because as soon as his mother got him alone, he'd get bombarded with questions. But being alone with Sandy—while usually something Tad craved—wouldn't be any better. Her social skills had kept her true feelings from surfacing, but she wouldn't hold back once they could converse privately.

Tad carried her bag up the shoveled walk, hoping his chivalry would win him some points. By her daggered look, he better prepare for an epic battle.

Chapter Eight

The sprawling home boasted red brick and white pillars. Sandy had never seen a home so beautiful, with so much land surrounding it. In the distance to the west, she found the boarding facilities, and she wondered how Tad could recreate in Three Rivers what his father had here. The barns and buildings at the ranch didn't come close to the operation here.

A coal burned in her stomach. She couldn't believe Tad hadn't told his parents he was bringing her with him. She couldn't understand why he'd do that, and the negative voice in her head hadn't stopped shouting once, despite her continued attempts to keep the conversation going.

Maybe he's not as serious as he claims to be.

Maybe he's embarrassed by you.

Maybe he's waiting to see if his mother likes you before committing.

The maybe's were endless, and they'd started to make Sandy's stomach feel like sour soup.

He led her down the hall. "My mom said you could stay in the guest room. I'll take the basement."

"Is the basement ready for you?" Sandy couldn't help the bite in her voice.

"It'll be okay."

"That's a no, because *she didn't know I was coming.*" The end of her sentence came out in a hiss.

Tad's stride didn't falter. "I'm sorry, Sandy. I didn't realize it would be a big deal." He entered the room and she followed him, closing the door behind them. A fissure had started at the airport, and she couldn't figure out how to make it stop cracking.

She folded her arms in a physical attempt to keep herself from falling apart. She'd already shown him some of her worst insecurities, and she didn't want to break down now, when this was supposed to be a fun trip to meet her boyfriend's parents.

Boyfriend rang in her head. She hadn't actually said the word out loud, hadn't acknowledged that coming here made him her boyfriend.

"Tad." Her voice broke, and she hated the weakness in it.

He gathered her in his arms, his warmth and scent

wrapping around her as effortlessly as his arms. "I'm sorry, Sandy."

She heard the remorse in his voice, felt it in his gentle touch, but something still wasn't right.

"I'm not very good at this," he said. "I've never brought anyone to meet my parents."

An alarm rang in her head. "Never?"

He shook his head, his grip around her firm. "You're the first. There's a lot about you that's a first for me. I don't know how to deal with it. I'm trying."

Panic welled beneath her breastbone. She needed to get away from him, out of the house, so she could think. He let her go when she stepped out of his embrace. "I need to think." She turned, yanked open the door, and fled.

"I can't believe you." His mother slammed a pot onto the stove. Her method of dealing with her emotions always came down to cooking. That, or scrubbing something really hard. She'd already scrubbed the kitchen counter until it gleamed.

"That poor woman. She looked like you'd dunked her in ice water." She pulled open the fridge and took out two sticks of butter. "Tad."

He looked up, his head almost too heavy to hold up. "What?"

"You need to go after her."

"I don't think she wants me to."

His mother unwrapped the butter and tossed them in the pot before turning to the pantry. "What were you thinking?"

He set his head back in his arms and moaned. "I don't know."

The smell of brown sugar told him she was making caramel popcorn, but he didn't look up at the thought of his favorite treat.

"She probably thinks you're embarrassed of her," his mother said, banging around the kitchen. "Or that you thought it was a good idea to introduce us, then panicked about it for some reason." She continued to muse over how Sandy might feel, but Tad tuned her out. He honestly hadn't thought it mattered. He'd just been trying to avoid his mother's questions. But her wrath and suggestions for how he'd hurt Sandy were far worse.

The tantalizing scent of butter met his nose, then sweet and salty came together. His mom finally fell silent, then she plopped onto the bench next to him. "Go find her," she said, her anger blown out. "Take this and go find her."

She held a zippered bag of popcorn toward him. "I

can see you like her, and it was pretty obvious that she likes you too. Are you serious?"

Tad shrugged. "Only started the relationship a few days ago." He hated saying those words in that order, but didn't love at first sight exist anymore?

"You've always known exactly what you wanted." She smiled at him. "It's good to have you home, Tad." She nudged the bag of popcorn closer and stood. "Now go find her." She left him in the kitchen with unsaid words.

He hadn't told his parents about the helicopter incident. He hadn't wanted to worry them, but now he realized that the people closest to him needed to know. They *deserved* to know. His mom and dad would want to help, the way Sandy did.

"Mom," he called. "I have to talk to you about something...." He grabbed the popcorn and went to find his mom and dad. If Tad wanted to find happiness, he needed to search for it, not just keep hoping it would show up in his life.

* * *

TAD EXPECTED to feel lighter after he told his parents about what had happened over the Grand Canyon, after he said he was quitting, after he confessed he was moving to Three Rivers. But as he took the keys to his father's truck and headed out into the bitter Wyoming winter, at least fifty pounds had settled on his shoulders.

He needed to find Sandy. Needed to apologize. Needed her to forgive him.

Tad didn't think he could make her understand. *He* didn't even understand why he hadn't told his parents he was bringing a beautiful, talented woman home with him. Or maybe because she was beautiful and talented and successful, he hadn't mentioned her.

And though his mother's caramel popcorn could charm anyone, he wasn't sure it would win over Sandy.

"But it has to," he muttered as he headed down the only road that led to town. He couldn't believe Sandy had walked this road. His fingers ached from the cold and he was in a truck with the heater blowing.

He passed his parents' nearest neighbor, and something screamed in his mind. He slammed on the brakes and put the truck in reverse. After pulling into their driveway, he approached the house.

George, the patriarch of the family, came out on the porch as Tad pulled up and parked. He got out of the truck, wondering how many people needed to know of his mistake before this day ended.

Apparently one more.

"She didn't want to come in." George leaned

against his porch railing. "Said she'd walk around the barn."

Tad nodded his thanks and headed around the house to the barn, his steps slowing the closer he got. The barn door stood ajar, and he pushed it open to find warmer air, scented with horseflesh.

He took a deep breath, remembering how much he loved the gentle animals. "Sandy?" His voice came out low, like he didn't want to spook her.

She didn't answer, and he headed down the aisle. Most of the stalls were closed, but a couple down on the end had horse heads poking out of them. He went that way, stepping lightly so as to not make any sound. The horses knew of his presence, but the soft sniffling coming from the tack room testified that Sandy did not.

"Just go back," she said, her voice tinny and small. It made Tad's heart pinch when it pulsed. "He said he's falling in love with you, and that wasn't a lie." She sniffled, and something moved in the tack room. "At least it didn't sound like it was, but—"

"It wasn't." Tad stepped into the doorway.

Sandy startled and looked at him with terror until she realized who he was. Her mouth opened, but nothing came out.

"It wasn't a lie." Tad sighed and moved to sit next to her on a wooden crate. "Would you believe that men are sometimes stupid? That we do things that we don't know matter, and then when we find out that they do matter, well, their mothers make caramel popcorn." He held out the bag of sweets.

"Sandy, I'm sorry. I've said it before, and I'll say it everyday until you forgive me." Tad's hands felt so heavy attached to the end of his arms. They hung between his knees, and his head bent in the same direction.

"Men do stupid things, huh?"

"And we don't even know why." He shook the bag of caramel popcorn. "You really should have some of this. It's amazing."

She took the bag and opened it, selecting a few kernels and popping them into her mouth. She moaned. "Oh, my goodness. This is like magic." She took another bite.

A measure of happiness flowed through Tad. At least Sandy wasn't crying, and she was talking to him.

"Is this a story that we'll tell at parties in a few years?"

The bag crunched as she fisted the top of it. "A few years?"

Tad inhaled, praying for that same strength and courage he'd used to tell his parents about his problems. "Sandy, I want to be with you. Not just today. For always." He exhaled. "So I'm hoping you'll forgive me, and that this will become a story that we'll laugh about as we tell other people about it. Not right now, or anything. But, you know, years from now."

Moments passed, but Tad didn't feel the same level of anxiety he had earlier. "Tad, I have some issues. You know, self-esteem issues."

A chuckle rose through his chest and out his throat. He lifted his arm and put it around Sandy's shoulders. "Honey, I have a lot of issues myself." He pressed his lips to her temple. "What a pair we make, right?"

She snuggled into him. "I've never really been part of a pair."

He inhaled her hair, recalling the bitterness in her voice when she'd told him about her many dating adventures. "I know, baby. But you are now."

She sighed, and Tad's muscles relaxed. He hoped he wouldn't do anything else that would hurt Sandy for a good, long while. He leaned back and tipped her face up to his so he could kiss her, wanting the way he felt about her to infuse his kiss.

Chapter Nine

Sandy walked into church on Sunday by herself, only because Tad had insisted on going out to the ranch to "check something" in the boarding stables he planned to use the following day. He'd promised to be back in time for church, and Sandy checked her watch.

He had four minutes.

She sat in from the end of the pew, her head held high as she tried to ignore the curious looks of the older ladies in town. It mostly worked, though Sandy still needed time to believe that someone wanted to be part of her life. Whenever she doubted, she basked in Tad's beautiful words and lost herself to memories of his heated kiss in the barn. Just thinking about it made her internal temperature spike.

Pastor Scott stood up, and Sandy looked over her shoulder. Tad hurried through the door, spotted her, and slid into his spot beside her. "Hey, sorry." He drew her close to him and pressed a kiss to her cheek.

Peace like Sandy had never known before—at least in Three Rivers—spread through her core, radiating through her whole body, coating each cell.

And though Tad had only been in town for ten days, Sandy knew she was in love with him. Her spontaneous smile could've rivaled the sun in its brightness.

"It's good to see you smile," he whispered.

She glanced up and kissed him quickly. "It's good to have something to smile about."

The End

Read on for a sneak peek at the next book in the Three Rivers Ranch Romance™ series - **ELEVEN YEAR REUNION!**

Sneak Peek! Eleven Year Reunion Chapter One

The sun had never looked so bright to Grace Lewis. Of course, she rarely saw the sun rise, what with arriving at work by three a.m. for the past several years. *The life of a pastry chef,* she thought as she turned out of her driveway and headed north.

She drove slowly, not wanting to arrive out at Three Rivers before everyone else. But she already knew she would. She'd been up since three a.m.—old habits and all that. She'd baked a loaf of bread that now rode shotgun next to her and would become lunch once noon rolled around.

By then, Grace would be ready for her afternoon siesta, but she didn't expect to be done in the kitchen that early. Heidi Ackerman had promised it would be a long day of baking, tasting, tweaking, and testing.

Grace couldn't be more excited.

She eased up on the gas pedal when she realized her enthusiasm over today's adventures had caused her to speed up. She enjoyed the leisurely drive through the crisp fall air, her thoughts wandering.

And when they did that, they almost always journeyed down south to Dallas. A frown tugged at Grace's mouth, and she did her best to straighten her lips again. So she failed in Dallas. Big deal. Many cupcakeries failed on their first try. At least that was what her instructors had warned the group of pastry chefs that had graduated from the Pastry and Baking School at New York's Institute of Culinary Education.

Still, Grace had thought sure she'd outbake the odds. She'd moved back to Dallas, gotten up at two a.m. for weeks perfecting her cupcake recipes. She painted the shop. Ordered the tables and display cases. Saw to every detail.

She'd made it eight months before admitting she couldn't put another month's rent on her credit card.

"Don't focus on that," she coached herself as she continued down the two-lane highway. She didn't want her thoughts to spiral right before she had to rely on her sharp wit and impeccable palate. If she allowed herself to continue down that particular train of thought, she'd end up obsessing over how she should've chosen a better location or entered more contests or started out of her kitchen before trying for retail space.

As the miles and minutes passed, she refocused her thoughts on the blessings that had led her to Three Rivers. Her friendship with Chelsea Ackerman—now Chelsea Marshall with two kids and a quiet life on a ranch she'd never wanted—made Grace smile.

It also reminded her of the boy she'd left behind in Oklahoma City. She banished those thoughts before they could even take root, beyond relieved when she saw the sign indicating a left turn for Three Rivers Ranch up ahead.

She maneuvered onto the dirt road, wishing she'd considered what the drive out to the ranch would do to her little car before she'd taken the job with Heidi. But it didn't matter. She wasn't in Dallas anymore and she still had the opportunity to work with baked goods. She'd be Heidi's head pastry chef any day, under any road conditions.

Grace pulled around the corner and the homestead Chelsea had described spread before her. Two homes, sprawling yards, a facility with a beautiful sign that read "Courage Reins," and new construction going in on the west side of the road. She passed that first, noticing that the construction workers were already out and busy.

Of course they would be, she thought. They didn't want to work in the Texas heat any longer than necessary, though it was October and starting to cool off.

She parked where Heidi had instructed, noting that she was indeed the first to arrive. Not wanting to wait in the car, she got out and took a deep breath of clean, ranch air. Chelsea had told her there was nothing like it—and Grace had to agree.

With a smile flirting with her lips, she headed for the homestead that would be Heidi's test kitchen for the next several weeks. Her son, Squire, now lived in the homestead, but his wife, Kelly, had insisted that Heidi come out and use the large kitchen to test her recipes. After all, Heidi's condo in town wasn't fit for four women to be baking in at the same time.

With no one but the cowhands and the construction crew stirring, Grace skirted the perimeter of the yard, thinking she'd take a short walk out to the fields and back. Someone surely would show up by the time she returned.

She noticed the calving stalls and chicken coops to her right. Beyond them lay the silos and a couple of barns and way down on the end, a large, portable building. Behind all of that sat a row of cabins, presumably for the cowboys who worked the ranch.

To her left sat the homestead, with its sweeping lawn and full vegetable garden, along with an obviously new swing set and shed. The tamed land eventually gave way to the wild range, and Grace paused on the edge of the two pieces. She felt the same as the waving prairie grasses—without shape or form or worry or care. At the same time, she longed to be molded and cultured into something beautiful. Longed to be needed. Longed to be successful.

She turned back to the homestead, wishing she knew how to become the person she wanted to be. She'd prayed for help, for guidance, for answers.

And God had sent her to Three Rivers to test recipes with a retired woman who wanted to open a bakery in town. A woman who had explained to Grace that she'd given up her dream of owning a bakery almost thirty-five years ago.

Grace took another deep breath as she heard Heidi tell her that she hadn't really given up the bakery. God had promised her she'd have it one day. She'd decided to trust in Him, and Grace admired the older woman's patience and faith.

She stuffed her hands in her pockets as she headed for the house. Heidi had told her to take the steps up to the deck and enter through the French doors. As she aimed herself in that direction, something glinted out of the corner of her eye.

Around the steps, under the deck, waited a patio. And on that patio, a guitar rested in a rocking chair.

Her fingers suddenly itched to play. She hadn't taken her guitar to New York with her, and she'd abandoned the instrument completely as she struggled to launch her cupcakery. But now....

Her feet seemed to change direction without instruction from her brain. She picked up the guitar, a small thread of guilt pulling through her, and sat on the edge of the rocker. Her fingers found the strings easily, pressed chords from muscle memory, and she began to play.

She'd hummed her way through her favorite tune, and was gearing up to sing the lyrics when someone said, "What do you think you're doing?"

Grace almost dropped the guitar. She fumbled it, her hands finally finding purchase on the neck and saving it from clattering to the cement.

Good thing, too, because she didn't think the glowering cowboy standing on the steps she'd come down would've appreciated her dropping his guitar. He definitely didn't need to vocalize that he owned it. His offensive stance and folded arms said that.

"I'm—I'm sorry." Grace stood and replaced the guitar in the rocking chair. The man continued to glower, his square jaw boxy and tight. "I was waiting for Heidi to show up, and I just saw your guitar, and—it's a real fine instrument. You must take good care of it."

Of course, leaving it outside in a chair didn't testify of

such things, but Grace swallowed those words. She wished she had her own cowboy hat to cover her hair and eyes, or that he would move so she could scamper past him and get upstairs and into her safe place: the kitchen.

"What song was that?" He didn't sound like he was about to snap, and the muscles in Grace's neck relaxed.

"Just something my daddy used to sing."

"I've heard it before."

Grace really didn't think so, but she didn't want to argue with the cowboy. He seemed so tall and imposing, standing on the third step as he did. And she was a tall woman at nearly five-feet-ten-inches.

His arms relaxed; his hands fell to his sides.

"You work here?" she asked.

"Workin' on the new horse training facilities."

Ah, so he was a carpenter. Grace had a soft spot for woodworkers—the boy she'd known in Oklahoma City had been a builder. Or at least his daddy had been, and Jon was set to take over the business once his dad was ready to retire.

Grace once again wiped the memories from her mind. It wasn't uncommon for her to think of what might've been with Jonathan Carver. She'd been infatuated with him, overjoyed to go to the homecoming dance with him, and then devastated when her family moved to Dallas before she could really find out if she and Jon were a match.

She had only been seventeen at the time, but still. Something about him had stuck with Grace through all these years.

Moving forward to go past him, she said, "Well, I should—"

He stepped in front of her. "Grace Lewis?"

She peered up into his face, searching for his identity. His dark blue eyes and strong features could've belonged to anyone. He swept his hat off his head to reveal dark brown hair—with a sliver of white in the front.

Her heart tripped over itself, then catapulted into her throat. "Jon?"

JONATHAN CARVER STARED at Grace Lewis, the girl he'd just started to fall for as a senior in high school when her family had moved. A slow grin stretched across his face. "It is you! I knew I'd heard that song before."

Without thinking, without considering, he stepped down to the patio and engulfed her in a Texas-sized embrace. Though she was tall, he still had a few inches on her, and her head fit nicely against his chest, right below his neck.

Suddenly everything about Three Rivers didn't

seem so distasteful. He'd come here against his will, because he worked well with Brett Murphy and he needed the money. But he didn't like Texas and wasn't planning on staying once the job was done. Problem was, nothing in Oklahoma City called to him either.

He'd been drifting for a few years, and he knew it. Didn't know how to anchor himself though. Didn't know if he cared to.

Heat bolted through him as Grace laughed and brought her hands sliding up his back. "It's so good to see you."

He stepped away, very aware of how hard his nerve endings had started firing. It felt as though the temperature had shot through the roof in only a few seconds.

"What are you doing here?"

She pointed up, toward the deck. "I told you. I'm here to test recipes with Heidi."

"Right," he said, listening now. He hadn't before, because his fury at seeing a woman fondling his guitar had deafened him momentarily. "She's startin' up a bakery, right?"

"In the new year," Grace said, her slate blue eyes dancing with light. He wanted to reach out and tug on one of her sandy blonde curls, the way he had in history class all those years ago. He fisted his fingers instead.

"I'm her head pastry chef," Grace continued, a note of pride in her voice.

Jon grinned at her. "You go to school the way you wanted to?"

"In New York and everything."

"That's real great, Gracie."

She stiffened at the childhood endearment, and Jon's smile faltered. His confidence plummeted, and he suddenly wanted to collect his guitar and head inside for his cup of coffee. "Well, I should go."

"Oh." She shuffled sideways. "Okay."

He grabbed his guitar as he passed the rocking chair, all thoughts of bringing his coffee to the patio and playing while his morning off slid on by vanishing with the presence of Grace. He wasn't sure why he was running away, only that he didn't want to play catch-up right now.

He paused at the door leading to the basement, where he temporarily lived with Brett. He turned back to Grace. "It was real good to see you."

She smiled at him, driving his pulse to near erratic proportions. "You too, Jon."

He nodded and slipped inside, his thoughts volleying around his mind with the speed of a bullet. He couldn't make any of them settle long enough to do more than breathe and walk. The door snicked closed behind him, and he forced himself to move into the galley kitchen to the right.

Don't look back, don't look back, he told himself as he reached for the coffee pot and poured himself a cup with slightly shaking hands.

By the time he added sugar and brought the mug to his lips, he allowed himself to glance out the glass door.

Grace had gone.

Relief and regret flowed through his bloodstream simultaneously. *Really?* He aimed the question toward the heavens. He hadn't wanted to come to Three Rivers. Made that clear to everyone. His parents. Brett. God.

But, in the end, he'd come, because he'd felt like maybe in Three Rivers he could find the piece of his life that had been missing.

He just hadn't expected it to be Grace Lewis.

Is that why you led me here?

God stayed strangely silent this time, which only unsettled Jon further.

A COUPLE OF HOURS LATER, the scent of chocolate filled the basement. Probably the whole ranch. Jon had steadfastly refused to leave the couch, where a sports reel had been playing for hours. His coffee had long gone cold and his stomach roared with the want of baked goods.

He'd heard footsteps in the kitchen above him for hours, but now he heard them moving down the stairs. Sure enough, a knock sounded on the door next to the kitchen.

"Come in," he said, thinking of how he would've acted if the person on the other side of the door had been Kelly. In fact, she regularly brought dinner down to him and Brett and neither of them got off the couch for her.

Jon knew, though, as soon as the door opened, that the bearer of delicious food was not Kelly.

"Heidi wanted me to bring some samples around." Grace perched on the edge of the couch, a plate over-flowing with three different types of brownies. His mouth watered, and not just from the sight of the chocolatey goodness.

But from the woman holding it. Her skin held the hint of the summer sun's kiss, and he wanted nothing more than to touch it. His gaze settled on her lips as he wondered if she'd taste as sweet as the concoctions she'd brought.

"Jon?"

He blinked and snapped himself out of his fantasies. "Which do you recommend?"

"You should try them all." Her eyes held that

mysterious sparkle, the one that had first captured his attention in high school. Memories flooded him now. Memories he'd only been containing behind a thin wisp of plastic wrap because Grace wasn't physically in the room with him.

"Which first?" he ground out through a tight throat.

"The German chocolate is my favorite." She extended the plate closer to him, and he selected a particularly gooey brownie.

As he bit into it, he definitely decided that life in Three Rivers had just improved drastically.

* * *

Read ELEVEN YEAR REUNION, the next book in the Three Rivers Ranch Romance™ series! Scan the QR code below to find it.

Second Chance Ranch: A Three Rivers Ranch Romance™ (Book 1): After his deployment, injured and discharged Major Squire Ackerman returns to Three Rivers Ranch, wanting to forgive Kelly for ignoring him a decade ago. He'd like to provide the stable life she needs, but with old wounds opening and a ranch on the brink of financial collapse, it will take patience and faith to make their second chance possible.

Third Time's the Charm: A Three Rivers Ranch Romance™ (Book 2): First Lieutenant Peter Marshall has a truck-load of debt and no way to provide for a family, but Chelsea helps him see past all the obstacles, all the scars. With so many unknowns, can Pete and Chelsea develop the love, acceptance, and faith needed to find their happily ever after?

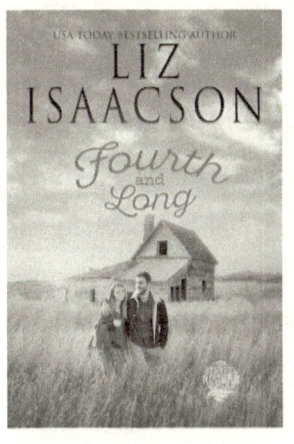

Fourth and Long: A Three Rivers Ranch Romance™ (Book 3): Commander Brett Murphy goes to Three Rivers Ranch to find some rest and relaxation with his Army buddies. Having his ex-wife show up with a seven-year-old she claims is his son is anything but the R&R he craves. Kate needs to make amends, and Brett needs to find forgiveness, but are they too late to find their happily ever after?

Fifth Generation Cowboy: A Three Rivers Ranch Romance™ (Book 4): Tom Lovell has watched his friends find their true happiness on Three Rivers Ranch, but everywhere he looks, he only sees friends. Rose Reyes has been bringing her daughter out to the ranch for equine therapy for months, but it doesn't seem to be working. Her challenges with Mari are just as frustrating as ever. Could Tom be exactly what Rose needs? Can he remove his friendship blinders and find love with someone who's been right in front of him all this time?

Sixth Street Love Affair: A Three Rivers Ranch Romance™ (Book 5): After losing his wife a few years back, Garth Ahlstrom thinks he's ready for a second chance at love. But Juliette Thompson has a secret that could destroy their budding relationship. Can they find the strength, patience, and faith to make things work?

The Seventh Sergeant: A Three Rivers Ranch Romance™ (Book 6): Life has finally started to settle down for Sergeant Reese Sanders after his devastating injury overseas. Discharged from the Army and now with a good job at Courage Reins, he's finally found happiness—until a horrific fall puts him right back where he was years ago: Injured and depressed. Carly Watters, Reese's new veteran care coordinator, dislikes small towns almost as much as she loathes cowboys. But she finds herself faced with both when she gets assigned to Reese's case. Do they have the humility and faith to make their relationship more than professional?

Eight Second Ride: A Three Rivers Ranch Romance™ (Book 7): Ethan Greene loves his work at Three Rivers Ranch, but he can't seem to find the right woman to settle down with. When sassy yet vulnerable Brynn Bowman shows up at the ranch to recruit him back to the rodeo circuit, he takes a different approach with the barrel racing champion. His patience and newfound faith pay off when a friendship--and more--starts with Brynn. But she wants out of the rodeo circuit right when Ethan wants to rejoin. Can they find the path God wants them to take and still stay together?

The Ninth Inning: A Three Rivers Ranch Romance™ (Book 8): The Christmas season has never felt like such a burden to boutique owner Andrea Larsen. But with Mama gone and the holidays upon her, Andy finds herself wishing she hadn't been so quick to judge her former boyfriend, cowboy Lawrence Collins. Well, Lawrence hasn't forgotten about Andy either, and he devises a plan to get her out to the ranch so they can reconnect. Do they have the faith and humility to patch things up and start a new relationship?

Ten Days in Town: A Three Rivers Ranch Romance™ (Book 9): Sandy Keller is tired of the dating scene in Three Rivers. Though she owns the pancake house, she's looking for a fresh start, which means an escape from the town where she grew up. When her older brother's best friend, Tad Jorgensen, comes to town for the holidays, it is a balm to his weary soul. A helicopter tour guide who experienced a near-death experience, he's looking to start over too--but in Three Rivers. Can Sandy and Tad navigate their troubles to find the path God wants them to take--and discover true love--in only ten days?

Eleven Year Reunion: A Three Rivers Ranch Romance™ (Book 10): Pastry chef extraordinaire, Grace Lewis has moved to Three Rivers to help Heidi Ackerman open a bakery in Three Rivers. Grace relishes the idea of starting over in a town where no one knows about her failed cupcakery. She doesn't expect to run into her old high school boyfriend, Jonathan Carver. A carpenter working at Three Rivers Ranch, Jon's in town against his will. But with Grace now on the scene, Jon's thinking life in Three Rivers is suddenly looking up. But with her focus on baking and his disdain for small towns, can they make their eleven year reunion stick?

The Twelfth Town: A Three Rivers Ranch Romance™ (Book 11): Newscaster Taryn Tucker has had enough of life on-screen. She's bounced from town to town before arriving in Three Rivers, completely alone and completely anonymous--just the way she now likes it. She takes a job cleaning at Three Rivers Ranch, hoping for a chance to figure out who she is and where God wants her. When she meets happy-go-lucky cowhand Kenny Stockton, she doesn't expect sparks to fly. Kenny's always been "the best friend" for his female friends, but the pull between him and Taryn can't be denied. Will they have the courage and faith necessary to make their opposite worlds mesh?

Lucky Number Thirteen: A Three Rivers Ranch Romance™ (Book 12): Tanner Wolf, a rodeo champion ten times over, is excited to be riding in Three Rivers for the first time since he left his philandering ways and found religion. Seeing his old friends Ethan and Brynn is therapuetic--until a terrible accident lands him in the hospital. With his rodeo career over, Tanner thinks maybe he'll stay in town--and it's not just because his nurse, Summer Hamblin, is the prettiest woman he's ever met. But Summer's the queen of first dates, and as she looks for a way to make a relationship with the transient rodeo star work Summer's not sure she has the fortitude to go on a second date. Can they find love among the tragedy?

The Curse of February Fourteenth: A Three Rivers Ranch Romance™ (Book 13): Cal Hodgkins, cowboy veterinarian at Bowman's Breeds, isn't planning to meet anyone at the masked dance in small-town Three Rivers. He just wants to get his bachelor friends off his back and sit on the sidelines to drink his punch. But when he sees a woman dressed in gorgeous butterfly wings and cowgirl boots with blue stitching, he's smitten. Too bad she runs away from the dance before he can get her name, leaving only her boot behind...

Fifteen Minutes of Fame: A Three Rivers Ranch Romance™ (Book 14): Navy Richards is thirty-five years of tired—tired of dating the same men, working a demanding job, and getting her heart broken over and over again. Her aunt has always spoken highly of the matchmaker in Three Rivers, Texas, so she takes a six-month sabbatical from her high-stress job as a pediatric nurse, hops on a bus, and meets with the matchmaker. Then she meets Gavin Redd. He's handsome, he's hardworking, and he's a cowboy. But is he an Aquarius too? Navy's not making a move until she knows for sure...

Sixteen Steps to Fall in Love: A Three Rivers Ranch Romance™ (Book 15): A chance encounter at a dog park sheds new light on the tall, talented Boone that Nicole can't ignore. As they get to know each other better and start to dig into each other's past, Nicole is the one who wants to run. This time from her growing admiration and attachment to Boone. From her aging parents. From herself.

But Boone feels the attraction between them too, and he decides he's tired of running and ready to make Three Rivers his permanent home. **Can Boone and Nicole use their faith to overcome their differences and find a happily-ever-after together?**

The Sleigh on Seventeenth Street: A Three Rivers Ranch Romance™ (Book 16): A cowboy with skills as an electrician tries a relationship with a down-on-her luck plumber. Can Dylan and Camila make water and electricity play nicely together this Christmas season? Or will they get shocked as they try to make their relationship work?

The First Lady of Three Rivers Ranch: A Three Rivers Ranch Romance™ (Book 17): Heidi Duffin has been dreaming about opening her own bakery since she was thirteen years old. She scrimped and saved for years to afford baking and pastry school in San Francisco. And now she only has one year left before she's a certified pastry chef. Frank Ackerman's father has recently retired, and he's taken over the largest cattle ranch in the Texas Panhandle. A horseman through and through, he's also nearing thirty-one and looking for someone to bring love and joy to a homestead that's been dominated by men for a decade. But when he convinces Heidi to come clean the cowboy cabins, she changes all that. But the siren's call of a bakery is still loud in Heidi's ears, even if she's also seeing a future with Frank. Can she rely on her faith in ways she's never had to before or will their relationship end when summer does?

Second Generation in Three Rivers Romance™ Series

Step back into the heartwarming small Texas town of Three Rivers! This beloved town has captured the hearts of 2.5 million readers and caught the eye of Sony Pictures, and now a new generation of cowboys and cowgirls is ready to take center stage. Scan the QR code below with your phone to check out this new series!

1. The Cowboy Who Came Home - featuring Squire's son, Finn from SECOND CHANCE RANCH!

Seven Sons Ranch in Three Rivers Romance™ Series

Meet the cowboy billionaire brothers at Seven Sons Ranch! Scan the QR code below with your phone to check out this complete series.

1. Rhett's Make-Believe Marriage
2. Tripp's Trivial Tie
3. Liam's Invented I-Do
4. Jeremiah's Bogus Bride
5. Wyatt's Pretend Pledge
6. Skyler's Wanna-Be Wife
7. Micah's Mock Matrimony
8. Gideon's Precious Penny

Shiloh Ridge Ranch in Three Rivers Romance™ Series

Meet the cowboy billionaires in the southern hills outside of Three Rivers! Scan the QR code below with your phone to check out this complete series.

About Liz

Liz Isaacson writes inspirational romance, usually set in Texas, or Wyoming, or anywhere else horses and cowboys exist. She lives in Utah, where she writes full-time, takes her two dogs to the park everyday, and eats a lot of veggies while writing. Find all of her books on her website at feelgoodfictionbooks.com.